Happy Holidays
& Warmest Wishes.

THE Duke's Christmas

USA TODAY BESTSELLING AUTHOR
ANTHEA LAWSON

THE DUKE'S CHRISTMAS
A SWEET VICTORIAN HOLIDAY TALE

ANTHEA LAWSON

Fiddlehead Press

Thank You,
Kickstarter Backers!

Adrienne Romani
Alex Harlequin
Alexandra Corrsin
Amanda Balter
Amanda Eschmeyer
Anitha Krishnan
Anonymous Reader
Billye Herndon
Bridget c
Carly Arave
Cate Dean
Cindy Carroll
D.L. Gardner
Dean Smith
Diane Kitevski
Eric & Kristin Brann
Eva Holmquist
Jen Desmarais
John Idlor
Joyce Engel
Karen Dale
Kate Donlon
Katherine Shipman
Keisha Marie
Lauren Freeman
Leslie Claire Walker

Leta Blake
Lorri Moulton
Louise Bergin
Lu
Marie Devey
Mary Jo Rabe
Mary Kennedy
Merrie Destefano
MF Caram
Michelle
Michelle L.
Mighty V
Monique Michaels
Pip Walker
PunkARTchick "Ruthenia"
Rebecca M. Senese
Ryan M. Williams
Serena M
Shanon M. Brown
Susan Colleen Browne
the gingerbreadman
Thorn Coyle
Two RomanticAppalachians
Valentine Jauner
Vickie Grider

CONTENTS

NEW YEAR'S FORTUNE

This one goes out to everyone in need of sweetness at the end of the year ~

CHAPTER 1

The scent of ginger and molasses filled the low-ceilinged kitchen as Miss Philomena Clarke—Mena to her friends, who were regrettably few and far between, seeing as how their family estate was isolated in Yorkshire—carefully removed the pan of parkin cake from the oven.

Mrs. Stewart, their longtime family cook, looked on, arms crossed over her stout belly.

"It's not right for gentry to be messing about in the kitchen, miss," she said, as though they hadn't had the same argument for years.

Though this would be the last. A pang went through Mena at the thought, and she quickly pushed the painful knowledge away. There would be time enough to give way to despair later. For now, there was gingerbread.

She inhaled deeply of the warmth as she set

the pan on the iron trivet atop the wide kitchen table, then looked at Mrs. Stewart.

"I know," Mena said, trying to smile. "And yet you indulge me."

"I suppose someone ought," Mrs. Stewart said with a sniff. "Whether you deserve it or not."

Sudden tears blurred Mena's vision and she blinked hard, hoping the cook would think the heat had gotten to her. The gruff old woman had always been kind, and the kitchen had always been Mena's refuge from the coldness of the rest of the baronial manor.

Not that Marston Mews was a particularly grand home, as such things went. Nothing like Dovington Hall, the vast and glittering estate of the Dukes of Beckford that lay on the far side of the village. In her memory, that estate was an enchanted castle, and the people who dwelt there lived happy and perfect lives.

But it had been a decade since her family had anything to do with the late Lord Beckford, his horrible wife, and their dreadfully spoiled offspring.

We were friends, once...

Before the gulf in their stations became so painfully clear.

It was true that Mena's mother was from the village and not born into the gentry, but that was no cause for the duchess to accuse her of theft. Mena had been ten at the time—too young to fully understand the complexities that had caused the rift between the families—but she was still incensed on her parents' behalf.

Although now that her father had passed, he was beyond caring for such things as social niceties and matters of *noblesse oblige*.

"Make sure Tommy doesn't get into the gingerbread before it cools," Mena said, slipping her hands out of the quilted oven mitts and laying them beside the pan.

"That boy's a scamp, make no mistake," Mrs. Stewart agreed. "But he's good lad with the horses."

"My cousin will keep him on, won't he?" Mena bit her lip and glanced at the cook. For that matter, was Mrs. Stewart's employment secure?

Mena hadn't thought to ask her mother which of the servants would be staying when Cousin Basil took possession of the estate. Until that moment, she hadn't thought to question the future of the staff. Not when her own fate hung so heavily, a ticking pendulum over her head, liable to crash down at any moment and crush her beneath its weight.

Come now, she told herself. *Being a governess or companion won't be so bad.*

Plenty of young women of good breeding and few prospects went into genteel service. And for every tale of mistreatment and woe, there were at least an equal number of pleasant circumstances to be found. Weren't there?

"A pity about Mr. Whittaker," the cook said, giving Mena a sympathetic look. "Who'd have thought he'd go down to London and never come back. Especially when…"

She didn't finish the sentence. She didn't need to. Everyone in the village knew that young Whittaker and Miss Philomena Clarke were going to make a match. Until—they didn't.

"Yes, well," Mena said, briskly removing her apron and brushing a sifting of flour from the black sleeve of her dress. "I'll be down in half an hour to check on the gingerbread."

She pinched her lips together, unable to manage even the merest smile, and marched out of the kitchen. Everything was dreadful, and not even her grandmother's secret parkin recipe could make the future sweet.

Lord Andrew Harrington, fifth Duke of Beckford and generally a lighthearted fellow, stared at his sister, aghast. Despite the cheery crackle of the fire in the parlor hearth and the festive greenery draping the mantel, he felt as though he'd been thrust outside into the frosty Yorkshire morning.

"Invite Lady Marston and her daughter to Dovington?" He shook his head. "Is this why you insisted I come speak with you? It's a preposterous idea."

Viola smiled, as if her suggestion had been nothing out of the ordinary.

"Consider it an act of neighborly kindness," she said. "The baron is dead now—forgive my bluntness, but it's the truth—and Mena and her mother are soon to be turned out of their only home. The cousin sounds quite dreadful, from what I hear in the village."

There was so much wrong with her words, Drew didn't know where to begin. He held his hand up and began ticking off his points, as if that would make Viola see reason.

"One," he said, raising his index finger, "the unfortunate event of the baron's death doesn't change the longstanding feud between our families. Or did you forget that the baroness and our mother are bitter enemies? Two, that young woman's name is Miss Clarke in this household, not Mena. And three, I can't believe you're going gossiping about the village like some common schoolgirl."

He shook his upraised fingers at her.

Unrepentant, Viola lifted her eyes to the cloud-painted ceiling. "I thought you, of all people, would welcome the chance to mend matters with the Clarkes. Must you sound so stuffy and duke-like?"

"I *am* a duke," he reminded her. "And why would I want to hold out a hand in friendship to the family that treated our mother so unkindly?"

"She started it," Viola said, as if that made a difference. "It's time we mend our fences. And you were always fond of Mena—begging your pardon, *Miss Clarke*—even if you won't admit it. Don't you remember what fun we used to have, especially at the holidays?"

"That was a lifetime ago," he said. "We were only children."

Unbidden, a memory of Mena flashed through his mind—the first time he'd teased his sister's new friend, the daughter of one of the nearby gentry. It had been autumn, and he and his younger brother, Theo, had climbed the biggest apple tree in the orchard. When Viola and Mena had come looking for them, they'd pelted the girls with apples. Mostly they'd missed, but he'd caught Mena a solid blow on the shoulder.

Her brown eyes alight with fury, she'd

stomped up to the apple tree, clambered high enough to reach his foot, and pulled hard. Unbalanced, he'd tumbled down, barely breaking his fall with the other branches, and landed, sprawling at Mena's feet.

"You are so fierce!" he'd said, laughing.

She'd set her hand on her hips and scowled. "Only to people who bedevil me."

Then she'd turned with a toss of her head, her blonde braid swinging behind her as she went to rejoin Viola.

That flash of temper had surprised him—he hadn't paid much mind to Miss Clarke, before. After that, though, he made an effort to tease her, just to see the flush of color in her cheeks, the spark of temper in her eyes.

Somehow, teasing had turned to camaraderie as they roamed the grounds of Dovington, getting into scrapes and being scolded by various members of the household staff. Often Theo and Viola tagged along, but sometimes it was just himself and Mena, building a secret tree house or stealing sweets from the kitchen...

"Well?" Viola asked, stepping forward and waving a hand in front of his face. "Will you invite them?"

"I hardly think Mother would agree." Suspicion stirred in the pit of his belly, and he narrowed his eyes. "Why are you so set on this?"

His sister gave him a studiously innocent expression. "I've no idea what you mean."

"Matchmaking again, Vi? You've no talent for it, if I recall."

The innocence fell from her face, replaced by impatience. "It's not my fault you can't see the charms of Lady Fenton, or the Misses Harding, or—"

"They are all charming," he said, unable to keep the weariness from his voice. "A bit too much so, frankly. It's clear they're more than aware of the advantages of becoming Lady Beckford."

He turned toward the fire, bracing one hand on the mantel. He'd hoped to escape the increasing pressure to make a match, at least over the holidays.

"Really, Drew—there is no woman in this entire country who's insensible of what becoming a duchess means. Is this why you insisted on coming to Dovington for Christmas? I did wonder if you were running away."

"We've always had Christmas here," he said defensively.

Viola gave a snort. "We haven't celebrated the holidays in the countryside for at least four years, if you hadn't noticed."

"You know what I mean. It's not the same in London." Their townhouse in Mayfair was pleasant, but it wasn't imbued with Dovington's happy memories. He glanced out the window at the dusting of snow lying over the garden and the rolling contours of the dales beyond. "You have to admit, it's peaceful here."

"Peaceful." His sister sighed. "You can't put it off much longer, you know."

"I wonder if the sleighs we used to drive are in working order," he said, refusing to rise to Viola's bait.

For one thing, he wasn't looking forward to marrying, and for another, it certainly wasn't up to his meddling younger sister to choose a bride for him.

"You're impossible." Viola slapped him lightly on the arm. "You still haven't answered me about inviting the Clarkes to stay with us over the holidays. It's the season of forgiveness, after all." It was clear she wouldn't let the matter rest until he gave her a satisfactory answer.

"Aren't they still in mourning?" he asked.

"It's been six months," Viola said. "Long enough that an invitation isn't too unseemly, especially in the countryside."

"Then when Theo arrives, and if he agrees, we can broach the idea," Drew said.

Three to one was the best odds against their mother, the duchess—though he didn't know why he was even siding with Viola in the matter.

"There isn't time." His sister took a few impatient steps back and forth in front of the hearth. "You know our feckless brother. He might not come at all, or if he does, it might be just as the clock strikes midnight on Christmas Eve. We must send the invitation as soon as possible, so that the baroness and Me—Miss Clarke—will have time to respond."

"They won't say yes, even if we do extend them our hospitality."

"So, you will write to them this afternoon?" Her eyes shone.

"*If* you can get Mother's consent, which I very highly doubt."

Viola simply raised her brows. "We'll see about that."

Then, grinning like a fox, she swept out of the parlor, leaving Drew to wonder what, exactly, he'd just agreed to.

CHAPTER 2

$\mathcal{M}$ena stepped into the parlor at Marston Mews that afternoon, where her mother had called a meeting of the entire household. Wan sunlight lay across the faded carpet and illuminated the anxious faces of the assembled servants. There were six of them altogether: Mrs. Taff, who was the house-keeper, along with two maids, Mrs. Stewart from the kitchen, John the groom, and young Tommy, who was fidgeting mightily with his cap.

Mena's mother, Lady Marston—now the widowed Lady Marston, Mena reminded her-self—faced the staff. As Mena entered, the baroness gestured for her daughter to come stand at her side.

"As you are all aware," she said once Mena had taken her place, "the new Baron Marston will be arriving with his family this evening. Is everything at the ready, Mrs. Taff?"

"Yes, Lady Marston. The rooms have been aired out, including the nursery. And Mrs. Stewart has planned a fine welcoming supper."

Mena's mother nodded. "I would like to thank all of you for your excellent service. No doubt the new baron will enjoy the same standard of courtesy and efficiency that you have given my family over the years. I'll do my best to help make the transition as smooth as possible before Mena and I depart."

The two maids shared uneasy glances, but the rest of the staff nodded. Mena kept her expression as smooth as possible, though it was impossible to seem cheerful at the prospect of being ousted from the only home she'd ever known. At least Cousin Basil had given them permission to stay through January, though her mother had already moved out of the baronial suite and into one of the smaller bedrooms. Mena would retain her own room until they departed Marston Mews.

And then?

That was the question that kept her awake at night, staring into the darkness above her bed. The future entirely depended upon the generosity of Cousin Basil, of whom she knew very little. From the letters he'd exchanged with her mother, she'd gathered he was a frugal fellow, much concerned with the state of the baronial finances.

She couldn't fault him for that interest, of course. Going from Devon farm holder to Yorkshire baron was quite the change.

He was somewhat younger than her mother, and apparently married with several children—how many, he hadn't said. But Marston Mews had five bedrooms and a nursery in addition to the baronial suite. Surely there would be room enough for all of them for the time being, even if the baron possessed a half-dozen offspring.

Mena's mother had expressed the hope to him that she and her daughter might be able to stay on at Marston Mews, or perhaps receive a bit of extra funds to help them settle elsewhere. Unfortunately, Cousin Basil hadn't seemed particularly keen on the idea.

They couldn't go back to the house in the village where Lady Marston had grown up, as it was now occupied by her younger sister and family and there was not a speck of extra room in the simple little cottage.

Which left them very few options, none of them good.

Lady Marston dismissed the servants, all but Mrs. Taff, with whom she needed to consult about the household inventory. Mena curtsied to her mother, then followed Mrs. Stewart to the kitchen.

"Your parkin cake came out lovely, as usual," the cook said. "I was hoping I might serve it to the new baron and his family."

"Of course." Technically, everything in the house now belonged to Cousin Basil, with the exception of Mena and her mother's clothing and jewelry.

Mrs. Stewart nodded. "We'll show him that Marston Mews has plenty to offer. Though are you certain you won't share the particulars of your gingerbread recipe?"

"You know it's a secret," Mena said, slanting her a look. "Passed down through the generations. It's practically the only inheritance I have, and I intend to keep it close."

The cook let out a gusty sigh. "One would wish your father had left you a better dowry, and more than eight pounds a year for you and your mother to live on."

Mena swallowed past the sudden grief in her throat. Not just for her father, but for everything they had lost.

"He believed matters were all but settled between myself and Mr. Whittaker," she said. "And no one expected a fever to carry my father off so suddenly."

She hadn't foreseen how being all but penniless would change her suitor's mind about marrying her, either.

Mrs. Stewart clicked her tongue against her teeth, but said no more on the matter, though her opinion was written clearly upon her lined face.

Eight pounds a year was a paltry sum. Lady Marston had investigated the possibilities, and discovered they could not even let a tumbledown cottage at the edge of the village for that amount—not with anything left over to feed and clothe themselves.

"We'll go to London," Mena's mother had said. "The city will surely offer more possibilities."

Cheaper lodging, at least so they'd heard. And more importantly, the agencies that provided governesses and companions to the upper nobility, where Mena planned to present herself for interviews and hope for the best. Lady Marston was too old for such, and even if she were not, a widowed baroness entering employment would be entirely too embarrassing for all parties concerned.

Once Mena found a situation, they would rent a comfortable little house for Lady Marston, and Mena would send all her extra wages to her mother.

"I can take in some handwork, too," Mena's mother had said. "Don't look so shocked—I don't mean mending. Perhaps some fine embroidery or suchlike." Something befitting a genteel lady, even if she came from common roots.

Mena hadn't argued, well aware of the difficult line her mother straddled. Once elevated to the gentry, society held certain expectations of a woman. Appearances were everything, no matter how impoverished one might become.

Oh, if only Mena had a brother!

He would've inherited, and then Mena and her mother wouldn't be in such a mess. The lack of an heir had been a constant dark cloud hovering over the family. It was the cause of the only time Mena had ever heard her parents quarrel.

"It's your lack of breeding," the baron had said, his accusatory tone penetrating the closed door of the baronial suite. "The Marston line has never had a problem producing sons. But just look at your parents—nothing but girls."

"If that is truly how you feel," Lady Marston's had cried, her voice choked with tears and bitterness, "then annul our marriage. Throw Mena and me out on the streets so that you might try again with someone from the gentry.

Someone more *suitable*. We shall leave tomorrow."

Mena had heard the wardrobe door bang open, and then her father's voice, low and contrite.

"Martha, wait. I'm sorry. That was wrongly done of me. I don't want you to leave."

Muffled sobbing, as though Lady Marston was crying into her husband's shoulder.

"I feel it as keenly as you," she'd finally said. "More. I don't want to be a disappointment to you."

"Hush. We'll try again. And if nothing else, I'll see to it that you'll be well provided for."

Mena didn't know what had happened to keep her father from upholding those words. Perhaps his solicitor had dissuaded him from changing his will, arguing there was still time for Lady Marston to produce an heir. Or per-haps the baron had simply put the matter off, thinking he would continue in good health for another several decades.

Whatever the case, Cousin Basil had inher-ited, and Marston Mews was no longer home.

THE EVENING AIR had turned a cold and shadowy gray when a messenger knocked loudly on the front door of Marston Mews. Too early for Cousin Basil to arrive, but Mena had been half watching out the window, and observed the man handing a letter to Mrs. Taff.

Was the new baron delayed? Mena couldn't decide if she'd welcome the news, or if postponing the inevitable would only make matters worse. Gathering up her skirts, she hurried to find her mother and discover what the missive contained.

Lady Marston was standing in the parlor, frowning down at the opened letter in her hand.

"What is it?" Mena asked, squinting to make out the seal imprinted on the back of the paper. It looked imposing.

Her mother glanced up. "An invitation from Lord Beckford to spend the holidays at Dovington Hall, of all things. What nerve!"

It took a moment for Mena to recall that the invitation hadn't come from the old duke, who'd passed some years ago. No, this was from his son and heir, Drew—who had teased her so mercilessly when they were children.

At least his siblings had been pleasant. She sometimes thought of Viola and wondered how her former childhood companion fared. Was she married yet? Betrothed? They moved in far different circles now, and Mena had lost track of the family's doings.

"An invitation to Dovington?" Mena came to stand beside her mother. "Are you certain it's not just for a party or somesuch?"

Lady Marston gave her an exasperated look. "I can read, I assure you. But here, see for yourself."

She thrust the letter at Mena, who scanned it with increasing perplexity.

To Lady Martha Marston and The Honorable Mena Clarke,

It is my pleasure to extend to you an invitation to spend the holiday season with my family at Dovington Hall. We hope you will consider letting bygones be bygones and join us during this festive time of year, as you did in times past.

Regards,

Andrew Harrington, 5th Duke of Beckford

"WELL." Mena eyed the page, as if by staring at it long enough it would begin to make sense. "Why ever would Lord Beckford do such a thing?"

"I haven't the faintest notion," her mother

said. "Not once in ten years have they extended an apology, let alone a hand in friendship."

"We're not going to accept, are we?" Mena couldn't tell if the sudden tightness in her chest was hope, or irritation that the duke had presumed to write them in the first place.

"Certainly not!" Lady Marston crumpled the letter and tossed it into the fire. "I can only think Lord Beckford was moved by some misplaced sense of pity or fleeting desire to help those less fortunate. As if we need his assistance."

Mena pressed her lips together and resisted the urge to snatch the burning letter from the hearth. Her mother spoke the truth. It was beyond strange for the duke to issue such an invitation after the long years of silence between their two households.

And to mention former holidays? Why, she'd all but forgotten they used to visit Dovington Hall during Christmas. Memories of laughter and sleigh rides and pelting one another with snowballs arose—hazy, as if viewed through fogged glass.

"Are you going to reply?" she asked.

"Though I would like our silence to serve," Lady Marston said frostily, "I will pen a short refusal. Later. For now, the new baron is due to arrive at any moment, and we must be ready."

No sooner had she spoken than Mrs. Taff bustled into the room.

"My lady," the housekeeper said, "Tommy reports that a carriage is just coming down the lane, headed for Marston Mews. The new baron is here."

Anxiety twisted Mena's stomach. The future was barreling down upon them, and there was no way she could fling herself out of its path. She only hoped she wouldn't be crushed beneath its iron-bound wheels.

CHAPTER 3

Three elegant silver candelabra cast warm light over the dining table at Dovington Hall as Drew and his mother and sister entered the formal dining room for supper. He waited for the ladies to sit in a rustle of taffeta skirts, then took his place at the head of the table. The head footman stepped forward to serve the first course—quail poached in white wine and shallots—while his underling poured golden Chardonnay into the crystal goblets set at each place.

"No word from Marston Mews?" Viola asked, running a finger around the base of her goblet.

"None." Drew looked at her. "I told you they wouldn't accept."

Their mother pinched her lips together. "I should not have let you convince me to lend my endorsement to your mad scheme, Viola. That family has ignored all our overtures in the past. Common rudeness—not that I expected anything less."

"I suppose it will keep the holidays simple," Drew said, tamping down his unaccountable regret at their lack of reply. Why should he care what Miss Clarke and her mother chose to do —or not do?

"Simple, at least until Theo arrives." Viola's smile was mischievous as she took a bite of quail.

"What are you saying?" Their mother leaned forward. "If Theodore plans to bring his ramshackle friends here unannounced, I'll send them packing right back to London."

"Oh, he's not doing that," Viola said.

"What, then?" Drew gave her a stern look.

"Nothing untoward or dangerous, I promise. It's just a holiday surprise."

"And has he seen fit to inform you of when he expects to arrive?" the duchess asked dryly. "Since clearly the elders of the family aren't worthy of such information."

Drew wasn't sure he liked being numbered among the elders, but there was no denying that the dukedom carried its own weight.

"Soon," Viola assured them.

"I'd hope so." Drew took a swallow of wine.

"Christmas is nearly here. Otherwise he'll miss the holidays altogether."

His sister gave a *tsk*. "There's always New Year's."

"I'll be going back to London on Boxing Day," Drew said. "The solicitors will have the year-end accounts prepared for me to look over."

Half of running a dukedom was tending to paperwork—and in the years since he'd inherited the title, Drew hadn't discovered a way to ease that burden. Other than by abandoning it altogether, which some gentlemen of his acquaintance chose to do. Foolishly, of course, as witnessed by the decline of their estates and fortunes.

But the Beckford legacy was well in hand: the home farms, the lavish London townhouse, the hunting lodge and second country estate, not to mention his younger brother's holdings as Viscount Thornton. Which, despite Theo's carefree ways, he seemed to be managing well enough.

For himself, Drew felt he was doing a fine job as Lord Beckford in every respect—except for the continuance of the family line. Which, unfortunately, his mother was nearly as quick to point out as his sister whenever the opportunity arose.

"Theo should be here tomorrow," Viola said, with an emphasis on *should*. "Even if we aren't to have any other guests, he'll liven things up."

"Perhaps next year we should open Dovington Hall for a grand holiday house party," Drew said, surprising himself.

His mother raised her brows. "When did you become so enamored of Christmas festivities?"

"I'd forgotten how much I like it here in winter," he answered. "We've had good times at Dovington. Why not share them?"

"That's a fine idea," Viola said, her eyes twinkling. "A Christmas ball! What fun."

He gave her a look. No doubt she was already hatching plans to invite all the eligible young ladies from near and far. But who knew—he might be engaged by that time, however unlikely, and then Theo would have to bear the brunt of their sister's machinations. His lips twisted in a wry grin at the thought.

EVENING WAS RAPIDLY DEEPENING into night, the air cold with the promise of coming snow as Mena and her mother donned their woolen cloaks and went out to greet the arriving carriage. Their handheld lanterns did little to beat back the darkness, and Mena glanced up at the constellations overhead. There was no moon, just the ice-white dusting of stars, as though the sky had already frosted over.

First to emerge from the carriage was a gentleman with large muttonchops framing a narrow face. Certainly that must be the new Lord Marston, who turned to assist his wife from the carriage. She paused, flicking a pinched, disapproving glance over the manor house, the assembled servants, and Mena and her mother waiting on the steps. Then, taking her husband's hand, she stepped down from the vehicle.

Immediately behind her came a tide of children, clamoring and exclaiming.

"Johnny trod upon my toe!" a girl cried.

"I did not," said a boy who looked only a little older. "Besides, it's your fault for sticking your foot where I was stepping."

"Must you two always squabble?" This from the tallest of the children, a girl who was perhaps eleven.

"I'm hungry!" a younger boy said.

"Me too!" echoed his little sister.

This outpouring was underscored by a baby crying as a tired-looking nurse emerged last, an infant in her arms.

"Oh, my," Mena's mother said under her breath. "That's quite a brood."

Mena was performing some quick calculations in her head. Six children, plus the nursemaid. The girls could take one of the spare bedrooms, the boys the other, and the nurse and baby would fit in the nursery. There was room enough for all of them, with a single guestroom left over.

"It will be a cheerful holiday," Mena said bracingly, though it seemed more likely that chaos would win out over cheer.

Her mother raised a quick eyebrow, then, smoothing her expression, stepped forward to greet the new baron.

"Welcome to Marston Mews," she said. "I am Lady Martha Marston, and this is my daughter, Miss Philomena Clarke."

"Mr. Basil...err..." His wife jabbed him in the ribs with one black-gloved finger, and he shot her an annoyed look. "That is, Lord Marston. And my wife Lady Marston, of course."

"Of course," Mena's mother echoed, and Mena dipped them a curtsey in greeting.

"This is the baronial manor?" Cousin Basil's wife surveyed the ivy-covered stone house with a disapproving frown. "Why, it's barely bigger than our farmhouse back in Devon. I was expecting something *much* larger."

"It's quite roomy inside," Mena's mother said, pasting a smile on her face that looked sincere to anyone who didn't know her. "We'd be delighted to show you around, once you've met the staff."

The new Lady Marston turned her censorious gaze upon the people arrayed beside the front door. The tip of Tommy's nose was pink from the cold, and the maids looked like they could hardly wait to scurry back inside, but John the groom, Mrs. Stewart, and Mrs. Taff stood stoically beneath their new mistress's gaze.

"Well." Lady Marston sniffed with displeasure. "I suppose the size of the house explains why you have so few servants. There is no butler? No ladies' maid?"

"Mr. Pimcoe was our butler, but he passed some years ago, and there was really no need to replace him," Mena's mother said, the tight smile still perched on her lips. "We don't stand on ceremony much here, as you'll soon find. As to a ladies' maid, young Sarah has a deft touch and will certainly be able to assist you."

Sarah, who was a somewhat flighty thing, shot Mena's mother a panicky look. Still, Mena thought, if she could settle, she'd do well enough.

"I see." The new Lady Marston's tone was cool.

Mena tried to keep her growing dislike of the woman hidden. It had surely been a long journey in a coach full of quarrelsome children, who were still bickering and complaining of hunger as they swirled about the doorstep. One couldn't fault the new baroness for being a touch out of sorts upon her arrival.

The staff was introduced and then they all trooped inside, where the noise of high voices amplified, ricocheting off the mahogany-paneled walls of the entryway.

"Quiet!" Cousin Basil bellowed, and the children fell silent. Even the baby stopped squalling mid-cry.

"Thank you, dear," his wife said.

"Perhaps we ought to begin with the nursery." Mena's mother led them to the main staircase, at the head of a parade that included the new baron and his family, Mrs. Taff, and Mena.

Tommy and the maids brought up the rear, bearing the first round of the family's luggage, which had been piled high on the top and back of the carriage. Six children and three adults made for quite a bit of encumbrance while traveling.

Mena's mother indicated the baronial suite, and the new Lady Marston finally seemed mollified by the fact that she and her husband would share a fine set of rooms. The nursery was located at the end of the hall, and the nurse agreed that she and the baby would be comfortable in the small space.

"I thought the rose room would do for the girls," Mrs. Taff said, opening the door of that bedroom. "And the blue room next door, for the boys. If you agree, my lady?"

She looked at the new Lady Marston, who nodded. "It will suffice. Now, where are the rest of the bedrooms? Is there another wing?"

Mena and her mother exchanged a look, the smile finally dropping from the widowed baroness's lips. A sense of impending doom settled like ashes on Mena's shoulders.

"There are three more rooms here." Mena's mother indicated the remaining doors on the other side of the hallway. "One is Mena's, one can serve as a guest room, and I have taken the other. But that is the entirety of the bedrooms."

"Oh dear," Cousin Basil said dolefully. "Where shall we put the others?"

"The...others?" Mena's mother blinked twice in quick succession.

"Yes—my parents are coming to live with us," the new Lady Marston said. "Their cottage is quite drafty, you see, and in much need of repair. And Basil's Aunt Hortense acts as the children's governess. We have engaged a tutor for the boys, as well, a Mr. Tipps. They should be arriving shortly, in the second carriage."

Mena couldn't stifle a small sound of dismay. Where would they possibly put everyone? The maids, the groom, young Tommy, and Mrs. Stewart lived down in the village, and Mrs. Taff had only a tiny bedroom of her own on the ground floor. Marston Mews had never been meant for a grand manor house, and so there were no servants' quarters. The attic was barely three feet high—tall enough for storage, but certainly not for people.

"The second carriage?" Mena's mother asked. "You didn't think to notify us?"

"And you didn't think to tell us that Marston Mews barely qualifies as a house, let alone a baronial manse?" Cousin Basil turned his heavy gaze upon Mena's mother. "I'd expected better from Marston Mews. Are there even mews?"

"There are," Mena hastened to say, as it seemed her mother was at a temporary loss for words. "Behind the house."

"Well, perhaps you can remove yourselves to that location," the new Lady Marston said with a flap of her hand. "We can't very well turn my parents out into the snow now, can we?"

"Or Aunt Hortense," her husband added.

Not to mention the tutor. Mena bit her lip. "The thing is, the mews are worse than a stables. They certainly cannot function as extra bedrooms."

She didn't mention the hole in the roof, the broken curricle, or the piles of gardening equipment and tools lining the walls. The small, musty building that had used to house the falcons of Dovington Hall had never been—and never would be—a place fit for human habitation. There wasn't even a single fireplace, for heaven's sake.

"I shall double up with Mena for tonight," her mother said, glancing at Mena in apology.

"Perhaps the younger children can go into the nursery, my lady?" Mrs. Taff asked, wisely deferring to the new baroness. "The older ones can share the blue room, and that would leave three bedrooms available for the others."

It was a solution—but only a temporary one. Mena and her mother couldn't occupy a single room between the two of them for more than a handful of days. And the children would need more than one bedroom and the nursery to contain the six of them.

"Tomorrow, Mena and I will seek out other

arrangements," Mena's mother said, with a confidence that Mena couldn't share. "Mrs. Taff, please delay supper until the second carriage arrives."

"Very good." The housekeeper nodded and bustled off.

The nurse shepherded the children away—quite a feat, in Mena's opinion—and the new baron and baroness withdrew to freshen up in their new suite.

Left alone in the suddenly quiet hallway, Mena and her mother stared at each other for a long moment.

"Will it be Dovington Hall, then?" Mena asked quietly.

"Certainly not." Her mother straightened, a steely look in her eyes. "No doubt the Pint and Plough inn will have rooms. I'll send young Tom down to the village to make arrangements, after supper. Now, come help me pack."

CHAPTER 4

$\mathcal{I}$t had snowed in the night, turning their corner of Yorkshire into a perfect winter scene. Unfortunately, that was the only good thing about the morning. The new snow hid the ruts and holes in the road as the cart jolted along, bearing Mena and her mother away from Marston Mews.

Bumping up on down on the hard cart bench was uncomfortable, Mena thought, gripping the edges to keep her balance—but not nearly as unpleasant as being displaced from the only home she'd ever known in the course of a single evening. She'd understood they must leave, of course, but to be turned out so abruptly was both maddening and quite deflating.

The cart hit another rut, throwing Mena

against her mother. Behind them, the stacked luggage wobbled. Turning, Mena made a grab for one of the hatboxes as it tumbled forward, barely managing to catch it before it dropped into the slush.

The further they traveled, the more the pristine snow changed to muddy slurry churned up by hooves and wheels. But perhaps it was better to see the grim reality. Though the blanket of white was beautiful, it hid too much, presenting to the world a façade of perfection that was far from the truth.

"Sorry, ladies," John the groom said after they'd endured another rough patch. "We'll be on the Beckford grounds soon, and the road's better there."

"Dovington Hall," Mena's mother said dispiritedly. "I swore we'd never visit there again."

In the end, however, there'd been no other choice.

Tommy had returned from the village with the news that the inn was full to the rafters. The innkeeper's wife had recently borne twins, and apparently her entire extended family had come to visit and exclaim over the infants.

Briefly, Mena and her mother had discussed going farther afield, but the roads were not good—as evidenced by their current slow progress—and even if they reached Harrowgate before nightfall, there was no guarantee they'd find rooms there, either.

"It must be Dovington," Mena had said to her mother early that morning as they packed up their belongings.

Wan lantern light flickered over the clothing heaped on her bed—most of it in half-mourning shades of black-accented gray, mauve, and lavender. It would be another several months before she emerged from mourning to don the few colorful gowns she owned. Those, plus a small pile of books and mementos, were all that would fit into her trunk.

Lady Marston straightened from her packing, one hand to her back.

"I told you last night, under no circumstances—"

"They *invited* us." Mena couldn't keep the edge of impatience from her voice. "I know you and Lady Beckford are no longer friends, but surely it's proof she no longer holds a grudge."

"A grudge! I'm the one who was wronged, if you recall. Can you imagine, being accused of stealing the duchess's sapphire necklace as though I were no better than a common thief."

According to the late Lord Marston, it had

been more an implication than an outright accusation, but Mena's mother had rightly taken offense.

"Perhaps this is their way of making amends," Mena said. "An apology, if you will."

"Ten years too late." Her mother shook her head, mouth set. "I won't accept it."

A sliver of gray light shone through the curtains, and Mena went to open them to admit the dawn. She paused, transported for a moment by the soft white coverlet drawn up over the landscape.

"Look." She thrust the curtains wide. "It snowed."

"Oh dear." Her mother joined her at the window. "That complicates matters. Perhaps it will melt soon. I'd hoped to travel some distance from Marston Mews."

"We needn't linger at Dovington," Mena coaxed. "Just a day or two—long enough to make other arrangements. You must admit, we can't stay here."

The sound of the baby crying echoed down the hall as the nursery door opened, followed by the clatter of running feet and high laughter.

"Quiet!" the new baron bellowed from the baronial suite, his voice carrying through the thick door.

"Quiet, yourself," a querulous voice called

back from the bedroom across the hall, where the baron's aunt was installed.

Mena's mother sighed, and Mena knew she'd won.

Now, though, as the granite columns flanking the drive to Dovington Hall loomed ahead, she couldn't help the twist of apprehension in her chest.

It's only temporary, she reminded herself. Besides, the Beckford family was the cream of the *ton*. No matter how awkward things might be, a veneer of social nicety would cover over the worst of the ruts and potholes.

Unlike the new Baron and Baroness Marston, who hadn't been able to contain their satisfaction as the widowed baroness and her daughter departed Marston Mews.

"Take care," Mrs. Stewart had whispered, giving Mena a quick embrace at the kitchen doorway when she'd gone to say goodbye.

Even the stoic Mrs. Taff had sniffed once or twice, though she'd blamed the cold morning for it.

And then Mena and her mother had left, all their earthly possessions stacked in the cart behind them as they set off into the unbearably bright light of a new day.

❄

DREW GRINNED as he spurred his horse down the evergreen-lined drive. Despite the butler's raised brows, he'd gone out without a hat, and now reveled in the feeling of the wind ruffling his dark hair.

It was a glorious morning, crisp and full of possibility, and he felt like a boy again. Gone were the burdens of being a duke: the necessities of estate management, the pressure to find a suitable bride, the strict code of behavior that wrapped about him so tightly that sometimes he felt he could scarcely breathe.

Or perhaps that was simply the dense and sooty air of London.

At any rate, it was grand to be out of the city, out from under the mountains of paperwork and responsibilities. He ought to repair to the country much more frequently. It was good for the soul.

The sun threw diamond sparks from the new snowfall, and the dark green firs beside the road carried a perfect frosting of white. The faint sound of church bells drifted from the distant village. Glee rose in him in an irrepressible bubble. For the moment, he was free.

His laughter plumed into the chilly air, and he laughed again just to see it—mirth made visible. The gelding under him pulled at the reins, and Drew let him run. Leaning forward into the bite of the wind, he let out a whoop as the trees flashed past.

They rounded the curve in the drive—and nearly ran over a heavily laden cart drawn by a stocky horse. The driver and two women occupied the bench, their expressions startled as he barreled down upon them.

"Whoa!" Drew cried, pulling on the reins.

His mount neighed sharply and reared, and Drew had to fight to keep his seat. The cart horse halted with a sudden jerk, and the pile of luggage in the cart teetered precariously.

The younger woman lunged to catch it, but she was too late. With a series of thumps, hatboxes and valises tumbled to the snowy ground.

"Oh dear!" the older woman exclaimed.

The younger one leaped from the cart in a swirl of purple skirts and faced Drew, hands on her hips.

"How careless!" she said, righteous anger snapping from her brown eyes. "You nearly ran us over, sir."

Drew finished wrestling his mount into obedience, and dismounted. He reached to doff his hat, then belatedly recalled he wasn't wearing one.

"My most sincere apologies," he said. "I wasn't expecting to encounter anyone on the drive this morning."

"Clearly," the older woman said tartly from her seat on the bench. Then she leaned forward, her gaze sharpening. "Heavens, is that you, Andrew Harrington?"

Belatedly, Drew realized whom he was facing. He blinked, looking from the widowed Lady Marston to the young woman still staring daggers at him.

Color rode high in her cheeks from anger, or the frosty air, or both. A lock of blonde hair had escaped her bonnet, pale against the dark fabric. Of course—they were still in mourning.

"At your service, Lady Marston," he said, bowing to the baroness, and then to Mena. "Miss Clarke, a pleasure to see you again. It's been quite some time."

An understatement, to say the least. The last time he'd clapped eyes on Mena, she'd been a girl in pigtails. Yet that sharp nose and stubborn chin were still recognizable, as was the annoyance in her velvet-brown eyes and the blush of temper in her cheeks.

That color faded, however, as she stared at him, eyes widening.

"Your Grace," she finally said, dropping him

a curtsey. For some reason, her formal manner stole the last of his high humor.

But of course she wouldn't greet him as her familiar childhood companion. A decade had passed since last they spoke. Not long after their families' falling out, he'd gone off to Eton, and thoughts of Miss Mena Clarke had all but evaporated from his mind. No doubt she'd felt the same.

The cart driver dismounted, bowed to Drew, and began scooping up the fallen luggage, brushing the snow off as best he could. Mena went to assist him, and Drew noted that, despite her sudden subdued manner, she made no apology for scolding him.

He would have joined them in retrieving the various satchels and hatboxes, but his mount wasn't trained to stand, and he couldn't impose upon the widowed baroness to hold his horse as if she were a stable hand.

"My lady," he said, inclining his head. "My condolences upon the loss of your husband."

"Thank you, Your Grace." She folded her gloved hands in her lap. "Let me offer the same in return, though belatedly, for the passing of your father."

It had been three years, and Drew still felt the hole in the fabric of his life where Lord

Beckford used to be. Most keenly, of course, when he was trying to shape himself to fit that empty space.

"I know it's trite to say so, but in my experience, time does ease the pain." He glanced to the luggage, now mostly restacked in the back of the cart. "Am I to understand you're accepting my invitation to spend the holidays at Dovington Hall?"

He could scarcely believe it. Oh, Viola was going to crow over him in victory, for certain.

The baroness sniffed, as though she wished to deny it. Yet there could be no other explanation for why they were on the drive to Dovington, riding in a cart laden with baggage.

"We are," Lady Marston stiffly admitted, after a long pause. "It so happens that Marston Mews is quite filled up with the new baron's family."

"They couldn't make room for you?" A flash of anger at the new Lord Marston went through Drew. "It's most ungentlemanly to turn a lady and her daughter out of their home. Especially at this time of year."

"Indeed," Mena said, wedging the last hatbox into the back of the cart. "And we're grateful for your invitation. Aren't we, Mother?"

"It was providential," the baroness said, which wasn't the same thing as a thank-you.

Drew let it pass. It seemed the ladies were not particularly delighted to be coming to Dovington—which would make for an interesting holiday. If not a comfortable one.

"Miss Clarke, allow me." Drew offered his hand to assist Mena up into the cart.

She laid her black-gloved palm over his and looked up into his eyes. One delicately arched brow rose.

"Were you always so dreadfully tall?" she asked.

"Only because you're so dreadfully short," he replied, unable to keep the amusement from his voice. Ah, this was the girl he remembered.

"I see you haven't changed," she said. "Even though you're now a duke." She stepped up into the cart, then pulled her hand from his and settled her black cloak around her.

"Mena, do be polite," her mother said in an undertone.

"No, no," Drew said. "It's well known that dukes have no sense of humor whatsoever. I'm working to become more dour, I'll have you know."

"Good," Mena said. "Perhaps you'll find that misplaced sense of gravity in the same place you left your hat."

He laughed, and saw her lips twitch with quickly suppressed amusement.

"I'll ride ahead to ensure the guestrooms are ready," Drew said, swinging up into the saddle. "We'll have wassail waiting when you arrive."

CHAPTER 5

Mena watched the Duke of Beckford ride away down the drive, his dark hair shining in the sunlight. It was shocking to her how quickly they'd reverted to their old patterns. The boy who'd annoyed her had grown up—into a man who still annoyed her.

"Well, I suppose there's no turning back now," her mother said as the groom clucked the cart horse into motion again.

From the moment the new baron had arrived at Marston Mews, there had been no going back to their old life, but Mena didn't point that out. Things were already unsettled enough without dwelling on their misfortune.

"The duke did say there'd be wassail when we arrived," she said, determined to make the best of things. "That seems quite hospitable."

"Hospitality or no, we won't stay a moment longer than we must," her mother said. "Although, I can say that from a gangly start, young Andrew has filled out well."

"Mother!" Mena shot her a look. "One shouldn't speak of a duke in such a manner."

Even if she'd been thinking along the same lines herself.

"Our families were friends, once," the baroness said, a shadow of regret crossing her face. Then she shook herself. "At any rate, it will only be a short imposition. We'll be off to Harrowgate as soon as the roads improve."

The groom shot her a skeptical look. "Begging your pardon, milady, but there's more storms on the way. And besides…"

"Spit it out, John," Mena's mother said when it seemed he wouldn't continue.

"I think you're best off waiting until after the New Year. The roads aren't good, and lodging's scarce over Christmastide. Always has been, unless you prefer a straw-filled stable."

"Harrowgate is hardly Bethlehem," Lady Marston replied tartly. "I've no doubt we can make some sort of arrangements."

Despite her mother's staunch words, Mena knew the groom spoke the truth. Indeed, despite the sunshine slanting through the low clouds, a snowflake drifted down and landed on her cloak. It lingered there a moment, a speck of white against the black wool, before melting away.

"Snowing again," John observed, flapping the reins.

The cart horse didn't speed up, but soon enough the stone walls of Dovington Hall rose ahead. Smoke curled from the multiple brick chimneys studding the roof, and the ranks of windows shone, reflecting the snow scattered over the sweeping lawn. The columns flanking the front door were wound with green garlands, and more greenery was draped about the doorway.

Despite the grand size of the building, the scene conveyed a homey warmth that sent a pang right through Mena's heart.

I will have a home again, she reminded herself. *Someday*.

As the groom pulled the cart to a stop, the door opened and two footmen hurried out to assist with the luggage. Right behind them strode the Duke of Beckford, accompanied by a tall young woman with the same dark hair and wide smile as her brother.

Mena immediately recognized Lady Viola, despite the years that had passed. Her long nose and wide-set, dark eyes were unchanged, as was her genial expression. Lady Viola was not one to fret, as Mena recalled. She'd re-mained ever-cheerful, even the time they'd fallen in the pond and emerged covered with mud and waterweeds—a memory Mena had nearly forgotten until that very moment.

On the seat beside her, the baroness stiff-ened, watching the door, but there was no sign of the Duchess of Beckford. Probably just as well. Mena bit her lip at the thought of that re-union. It could be nothing but fraught, and the longer it was postponed, the better. For all parties concerned.

"Welcome!" Lady Viola called as she and her brother came forward. "I'm so glad you've come. I could scarcely credit it when Drew told me he'd encountered you on the drive."

The duke halted beside the cart, offering his hand to assist Mena down. As his fingers clasped over hers, she tried to ignore the sudden speeding of her pulse. There was no reason for him to discomfit her so.

Hiding her reaction, she met his gaze squarely. "Did you also tell your sister how you spilled our luggage? I fear for the state of the hatboxes. Two of the lids came open and snow got inside."

Only a small dusting, however—hopefully not enough to ruin any of the contents.

She had only one hat she cared about, fashioned of blue velvet with an upswept brim and decorated with a profusion of pink silk roses. It was direct from Paris, and she'd purchased it in London last spring, when she and her mother had visited for a rare shopping excursion.

It was a reminder of a happier time, before her father had fallen ill. Before her then-suitor had gone off and, instead of returning to Yorkshire, penned her a most painful missive informing her that, due to her now muchreduced circumstances, he would no longer be courting her.

Those words still had the power to wound her, and she winced at the memory.

"Fear not." The duke, misinterpreting her reaction, pressed her fingers, then glanced to the footmen bearing the trunks and boxes into the house. "The servants will tend to things, and of course if something was damaged beyond repair, I'll replace it."

There could be no replacing the past, or mending her broken prospects, but Mena nodded anyway.

He released her fingers and turned to help her mother from the cart, and Lady Viola stepped forward with a warm smile.

"Miss Clarke! It's so good to see you. It's been ages."

"It has." Mena glanced at her mother, then

back to Lady Viola. "Is the duchess in residence?"

"Of course—she'll meet you in the gold parlor, after you and your mother have a chance to freshen up."

A slight reprieve, then. Not that the journey from Marston Mews through the village and up to Dovington Hall had been any great hardship. Other than the bit of snow and the spilled luggage.

"Do come in and get settled," Lady Viola continued, looping her arm through Mena's as though they were still the best of friends, and leading her through the front door. "Oh, this makes the holidays so much better than being trapped here with just my brothers for company."

"Is Theo—excuse me, Viscount Thornton—here as well?"

Mena didn't remember him nearly as well as his brother, the duke. Probably because Drew had always been the one to tease her mercilessly, while Theo was the quietest of the siblings. Not that he'd been entirely without mischief, but he usually followed his elder brother's lead in such things.

"Not yet." Lady Viola shot her a grin. "But he should be arriving in the next day or so—with a wonderful surprise."

"How wonderful it is remains to be seen," Lord Beckford said dryly from behind them as he escorted Mena's mother into the large entrance hall. "Viola will show you to your rooms, ladies."

With a bow, he left them at the foot of the grand staircase. The stoic butler took their cloaks, hats, and gloves without comment.

Mena glanced up at the sweeping mahogany banisters and couldn't help a small smile of memory. Those railings had provided a great deal of amusement one rainy afternoon. Until Mrs. Simmons, the dour-faced housekeeper, had caught them sliding down and given all four of them a resounding scolding.

It was true they might have cracked their heads open on the gleaming marble floor, but they'd all been careful to brace one another if the slider seemed to be losing their balance. And the boys hadn't let the girls slide from too great a distance, either, for fear their skirts might tangle and send them sprawling. As they mounted the stairs, Mena thought she could almost hear their long-ago laughter lingering in the air.

Lady Viola led them down the long upper hallway, then halted before a door.

"Your rooms, Lady Marston," she said, opening the door to reveal an elegant sitting room done up in shades of cream and gold. "I hope you find them comfortable."

A fire burned in the limestone-faced fireplace, and through another half-open door Mena caught a glimpse of an equally well-furnished bedroom, where two maids were already unpacking her mother's trunk.

The baroness stepped inside. "Thank you—they're lovely."

"Miss Clarke, you're next door," Lady Viola said, gesturing down the hall. "I'll show you. Once the two of you have freshened up, ring for the maid to take you down to the parlor."

Mena's mother nodded and closed her door, and Lady Viola led Mena to the next door over. Instead of standing back, however, the duke's sister accompanied Mena inside. Like Lady Marston's rooms, the suite boasted a sitting room with a small fireplace, a bedroom beyond, a dressing room, and a washroom.

Instead of elegant gilt and creamy stone, however, the color palette was green and silver. Large ferns set upon burnished pedestals softened the corners of the rooms, and the carpet underfoot was a motif of twining vines and leaves. The bed was hung with pale green draperies embroidered with silver, and the hearths were fronted with white-veined green marble.

The effect was soothing, and Mena felt the tightness in her chest ease. It wasn't home, but it was restful, even in its opulence.

"I thought you might like the Fern Suite," Lady Viola said.

"I do—thank you." Mena turned her attention to the duke's sister. "But why are you being so generous? Why the invitation?"

Lady Viola hesitated a moment, and then nodded as though she'd been expecting the question.

"Shall we sit a moment?" She went to one of the wing-back chairs drawn up in front of the hearth, then looked at Mena. "I'm glad Drew invited you—though to be quite honest, I didn't think you'd come, given the history between our families. Is the new baron truly so dreadful?"

Mena sighed and took the chair across from Lady Viola. "In a word, yes. His wife strongly suggested that my mother and I remove to the mews."

"The mews?" Lady Viola's eyes widened. "That's horrible. Might as well send you to the kennels. Or the chicken coop, for that matter. How could they?"

Mena gestured at her lavish suite. "Apparently, they thought Marston Mews was more along the lines of Dovington Hall. I don't know why they didn't think to inquire about the number of bedrooms before bringing along two carriages full of people."

"Two carriages?" Lady Viola shook her head. "I'm so sorry you were turned out of your home, though it's lucky for us."

"Why?" It was a blunt question, but Lady Viola had already avoided answering it once. "And don't try to pass it off as the holiday spirit. Not after our families haven't spoken in ten years."

"Well." Lady Viola glanced into the fire, avoiding Mena's gaze. "Though she won't admit it, my mother is terribly lonely. I've always thought that, given the chance, she and Lady Marston might be able to resume their friendship. The arrival of the new baron seemed the perfect opportunity, from what I heard in the village."

Mena's brows rose. "Indeed? And what might that be?"

The duke's sister made a dismissive gesture. "The usual gossip, really. No doubt you heard the same."

Although Lady Marston discouraged gossip among the servants, Mena *had* managed to wangle a word or two out of Mrs. Stewart. The cook had confided that Tommy's mother's second aunt's son was from Devon, very near

Cousin Basil's farm. Reports were that the new baron was a stingy fellow, and his wife puffed up by her own importance—both of which had proven true.

Mena wished that her mother had let the staff speak more freely, for then they might have discovered the truth about the new baron's extended family and the entourage about to land on their doorstep. Given advance warning, they might have been able to make better plans...

Suspicion wormed through her, and she narrowed her eyes at Lady Viola.

"Were you aware that the new Lord Marston intended to bring quite so many people to Yorkshire?" she asked.

"The innkeeper might have mentioned such a thing to one of our footmen," Lady Viola admitted. "His wife's sister came in from Devon, where half the county was abuzz with Mr. Clarke's change in status."

So, in addition to the number of people about to arrive at Marston Mews, Viola had also been aware that the inn was packed to the rafters.

"You knew!" Mena jumped up from her chair, agitation running through her. "You might have warned us."

She paced to the fire, three small steps.

When she turned back, apology shone from Lady Viola's eyes.

"I know," the duke's sister said. "But it wasn't my place, truly. The only thing I could think to do was to prevail upon Drew to invite you here."

"So this was your idea?" Mena waved her hand to indicate the Fern Suite and, by extension, all of Dovington Hall.

"Yes. I know it's small consolation for being thrust out of Marston Mews—but surely Dovington is better than the alternative." A defensive tone edged her voice. "Some people would have been overjoyed at receiving our invitation."

"Well, we are not," Mena said, letting her bitterness show. "My mother and I aren't whey-witted members of the *ton*, as no doubt your mother will remind you. I'm astonished she let us commoners set foot under her roof once more."

"Stop." Viola rose to face Mena. "I know you can be terrifically stubborn—it's why Drew admires you so much—but please, let's not quarrel. You and Lady Marston are here, for the time being, at least. Let's make the best of things, not the worst."

Mena blew an annoyed breath out through her nose. Her temper was riled, and arguing with Lady Viola was safer than confronting the bleakness of her own situation. But the duke's sister was right. Things were a proper mess, and having a spat with her host family wasn't going to make the visit any more pleasant.

"Truce?" Lady Viola held out her hand, her expression pleading. "I didn't mean to upset you. In fact, I'd hoped… Well, I'd hoped we could become friends again, too."

Her intentions seemed genuine, and Mena shook off the last of her irritation. Although she'd little hope that her mother and the duchess would be able to set aside their differences, perhaps their daughters could provide an example.

"Very well." She clasped Lady Viola's outstretched hand and gave it a squeeze. "I forgive you for forcing us to come to Dovington Hall, though it's a dismal pile of stone with no creature comforts whatsoever."

Viola laughed, as she was meant to. "I suppose you must endure the hardship. But I nearly forgot—my mother is waiting for us in the parlor."

Rather like a spider waiting for hapless flies, Mena thought.

"Oh, don't make that face," Lady Viola said. "Our mothers are civilized. And there will be wassail. Ring for the maid when you're ready to come down."

Even an entire vat of spiced and brandied cider wouldn't be enough, Mena feared, to set old enemies at ease. But there was no avoiding the confrontation ahead.

CHAPTER 6

"I have nothing to say to that woman," Lady Marston said to Mena as they descended the wide staircase.

"Then don't speak." Mena shot a look at the maid leading them to the parlor, and lowered her voice. "Honestly, Lady Viola talks enough for two people. And you can always plead a headache and excuse yourself."

"I've never had a headache a day in my life," her mother said. "And I'm not about to start now. I'll leave such foolishness to the peers of the realm."

"You're still Lady Marston," Mena reminded her, and was rewarded by a sniff in return.

The maid turned down the long corridor leading out of the entrance hall—another place echoing with memory. Mena and the other children had used to race back and forth, fiercely competing to see who was the fastest. Sometimes they ran in the gardens, but often they chose the very corridor she was now traversing.

Funny—now that she was at Dovington Hall once again, memories of her childhood assailed her at every turn. She hadn't remembered spending quite so much time with the duke's family, but apparently she had.

The plush Turkish runner underfoot was the same one she recalled sprinting across, and the grim-faced Beckford ancestors still stared disapprovingly down from the line of portraits mounted on the velvet-flocked wallpaper. She used to imagine them shaking their heads in disapproval whenever Mena beat their heirs—usually Drew, as Theo and Viola tended to take their rivalry less seriously—across the imaginary finish line.

They'd been quite evenly matched. Drew had the advantage of longer legs, but Mena moved more quickly. He never let her win easily, though he never bore a grudge when he lost, either. Even when she crowed about her victory.

To sweeten his loss, he would steal lemon-frosted teacakes from her plate, however—quite unrepentantly popping them in his mouth with a mischievous smile.

"Ladies," the maid said, opening the door to the gold parlor and curtseying as they passed through.

In the center of the room, the Duchess of Beckford sat in an ornate chair, perched as regally as though she were the Queen. Her gaze went from Mena to her mother, and her face tightened. The light glinting off the gilt accents in the room suddenly seemed harder—cold metal instead of soft gold. Only the smell of cloves and apple wafting from the bowl of wassail on the sideboard kept the room from being impossibly unwelcoming.

The duke stood next to the hearth, his expression markedly warmer than his mother's. Mena's eyes met his, and she suddenly recalled a snippet of his sister's words—ones Mena had barely attended to at the time.

"Drew admires you," Lady Viola had said.

Oh, but surely not. Still, a strange shiver went over Mena, and she was the first to look away.

The silence stretched out. Lady Viola, seated next to her mother in another scrolled and gilded chair, slanted the duchess a look.

For a moment, they were frozen in tableau —the duke's family facing Mena and Lady Marston—and Mena wished they'd never come. The gulf between them was too far to bridge.

Then the duke stepped forward. "For goodness' sake, Mother. If you won't greet our guests properly, then at least stop staring daggers at them."

Lady Viola quickly rose from her chair. "Come in, please. Do take a seat, and have some wassail."

She gestured them to the settee, and the footman stationed at the sideboard moved to fetch cups of wassail. The corners of the duchess's mouth pinched together, but she remained silent.

Mena surreptitiously prodded her mother in the back.

"Thank you, Lady Viola," Mena's mother said, then nodded to the duchess. "Your Grace."

Mena dropped their hostess a curtsey, echoing her mother's greeting. No matter how frosty Lady Beckford's behavior, they were still guests in her home.

The duchess coolly inclined her head. Mena and her mother settled, rather stiffly, on the settee. The footman handed around gold-chased cups of wassail from his tray, and Mena wrapped her fingers about her cup, grateful for something to occupy her hands.

"I believe it may snow again, tomorrow,"

Lady Viola said brightly. "How perfectly wintry the season has become. Drew, have you seen to the sleighs yet?"

The duke raised one dark brow. "The grooms tell me the broken runner on one has been mended and both vehicles are ready at our leisure."

"Marvelous!" His sister clapped her hands together. "Perhaps this afternoon we might all go out for a ride."

"I've no interest in gallivanting about in the teeth of a winter storm," the duchess said. "Though you may do as you please. You always do, despite what I say."

Lady Viola and her brother exchanged a quick look tinged with exasperation.

"Well, what about singing carols, instead?" Lady Viola said hurriedly. "Do say you'll play the piano for us, Mother."

"Must you foist your holiday cheer upon everyone?" The duchess set her untouched wassail aside and rose in a swirl of blue silk. "Excuse me—I believe I feel a headache coming on."

Mena's mother made a small sound of superior amusement, and Lady Beckford paused, fixing her cold hazel eyes upon her former friend.

"I commend you," the duchess said. "I understand a hardy constitution is considered a desirable quality in *certain* social circles."

The implication being that such circles were far inferior to her own.

Mena's mother opened her mouth—no doubt to make a scathing reply—but Lady Viola hurriedly rose and set her hand on the duchess's arm.

"Mother," Lady Viola said. "I truly think—"

What she thought, however, was left unsaid as the parlor door burst open and a dark-haired young man strode inside. His cheeks were ruddy from the cold, and Mena fancied he brought a gust of fresh air along with him.

"Hullo, everyone," he said. "Come and see what I've brought."

"Theo!" Lady Viola rushed forward to embrace her brother. "You're earlier than I expected."

"Or just in time." His gaze swept over Mena and her mother perched on the settee, then settled on Lady Beckford, who had paused midway across the room. "Mother."

He came forward and took the duchess's hand, bowing over it.

"Theodore," she said, her tone dry. "We have houseguests, as you see."

"Indeed." Theo nodded to Mena and her

mother. "Lovely to see you again, Lady Marston, Miss Clarke."

"Viscount Thornton," Mena's mother replied, and Mena nodded her greeting.

"Good to have you here." The duke smiled at his brother. "Dare I ask what kind of mischief you've dragged behind you from London?"

"The holiday kind, and not all the way from the city. Just from Knavesmire Wood."

"A yule log?" the duke guessed.

His brother grinned. "You'll see. Forgive the pun."

Lady Viola swatted him on the shoulder, and Mena felt a pang at the family camaraderie. She hadn't felt the lack of siblings so keenly for quite some time, but the warmth swirling about Lady Viola and her brothers made her feel as though she were standing outside a cozy house, looking longingly in through the lit windows.

"I've told the butler to fetch everyone's coats," the viscount said. "Yes, even yours, Mother. Come along. You can all return and finish your wassail later."

There was no resisting his enthusiasm, and so Mena found herself wrapped in her cloak and ready to step out into the chilly weather once more. Lady Beckford and her youngest son led the way through the front door, and then the duke, escorting Mena's mother. Lady Viola fell back to keep pace with Mena.

"I'm sorry for how awkward that reunion was," Lady Viola said in an undertone. "But never fear—Theo can bring our mother around better than anyone. I'll have him smooth things over. Dinner tonight will be better, I promise."

Mena wasn't so certain, but it was true that Viscount Thornton had coaxed his mother outside without too much trouble.

"Heavens!" the duchess exclaimed from the front steps. "Whatever is that?"

"It appears to be a tree, Mother," Lord Beckford said, clearly amused.

Lady Viola and Mena halted beside him, and Mena blinked at the sight of the enormous evergreen strapped to a cart outside the door. The tree was longer than the cart bed, the trunk protruding past the driver, the tip sagging off the back of the vehicle.

"What are we to do with it?" the duchess asked. "It certainly won't fit in any of the fireplaces."

"It's not meant for burning," the viscount said, "but for decorating. Surely you know that Christmas trees are all the rage, ever since the Queen and Prince Albert started installing one at the palace."

"Nevertheless, it seems a rather barbaric

practice," Lady Beckford said. "Do you truly intend to bring that monstrosity inside? There's no room."

"It will fit upright in the entrance hall, I believe," the duke said.

His mother turned a repressive look upon him. "Don't encourage your brother."

"Too late." He gave her an unrepentant grin. "Besides, this isn't the worst thing he's ever done. I say we welcome this new holiday tradition to Dovington Hall."

"I agree," Viola said. "What fun we'll have, coming up with decorations! As I recall, gilded almonds and various sweets are usual, and little presents, and, of course, candles."

"That seems hazardous," Mena's mother said.

"Indeed," the duchess said, and the two of them shared a brief look of mutual understanding. Then they seemed to recall their enmity, and the moment was gone, erased by Lady Marston's narrowed eyes and Lady Beckford's haughty sniff.

Mena let out a little puff of frosty air. Could there be any chance at reconciling the two? She fervently hoped so. Otherwise, they were in for an excruciating holiday, indeed.

❄

AFTER VIEWING THE TREE, the ladies retired to their various rooms, leaving Drew and Theo to coordinate the placement of the enormous evergreen.

"Could you have found a larger specimen?" Drew asked laughingly as the servants hoisted the tree upright in the entryway.

The room rose over two stories, and still the top of the fragrant fir nearly brushed the plaster cornices decorating the ceiling.

"I think I judged it perfectly," Theo said with a nod of satisfaction, before turning to Drew with a gaze full of questions. "What are the Clarkes doing here? Has our mother made up with Lady Marston?"

"Not entirely. Come, let's chat in my study."

The servants were circumspect, but it was always preferable to discuss family business behind closed doors.

"Brandy?" Drew asked as Theo settled in one of the leather armchairs beside the hearth.

"Yes, thank you. Take the chill off."

Drew went to the sideboard and poured them both a glass of the amber liquid.

"Inviting the Clarkes was Viola's idea," he said, handing Theo a glass and then taking the chair across from him.

"That doesn't surprise me in the least." Theo sniffed his brandy appreciatively before taking a sip. "I'd half expected to see all the eligible young ladies in the neighborhood gathered under our roof. Our sister seems quite intent on marrying you off."

"Well, it won't be to Miss Clarke, at any rate." Drew crossed his booted feet at the ankles.

His brother raised one eyebrow. "Why not?"

"Honestly, Theo—our mothers detest one another, for starters. And while Mena is a pleasant enough girl, her pedigree isn't exactly top notch."

"You sound even worse than Mother." His brother gave him a disappointed look. "When did you become such dreadful a snob?"

"When I became the Duke of Beckford, I imagine."

"And puffed up with it! If this is what the peerage has done to you, here." Theo mimed ripping something from his chest, then held his empty palm out to Drew. "Take your viscountancy back, for I certainly don't want it curdling my brains."

"You're impossible," Drew said mildly, refusing to show that his brother's words had stung.

Worse than the duchess? He swallowed back argument, the words as heated as the liquor against his throat. The Duchess of Beckford was notorious for turning up her nose at anyone she thought inferior—a tendency that had become more pronounced after her husband's death.

That was the root of the problem with Lady Marston, of course. And once the duchess had made up her mind, it was nearly impossible to change it, no matter how many years had passed.

"If you won't take Miss Clarke, then perhaps I ought to consider her," Theo mused.

Drew sat bolt upright. "Nonsense. She's leaving Yorkshire, at any rate."

"Bound for where?"

"London, I believe." He was uncomfortably aware that he knew almost nothing about Miss Clarke's situation. Not that it was any concern of his. He'd done as Viola had asked, and invited them to Dovington for the holidays. Beyond that, he had his own life to contend with.

"Do you remember the snowball fights we had, that one Christmas it snowed every day?" Theo asked with a half-smile. "You and Miss Clarke nearly pelted Viola and me into oblivion."

"You got your revenge, as I recall. An icicle tucked beneath the sheets is not a happy thing to encounter on a cold winter's night. Besides, you and Mena beat us in the sleigh race."

"Did you know you've called her Mena twice now?" Theo gave him a conspiratorial wink. "That sounds like a man besotted, to me."

Drew sputtered on his sip of brandy and set the glass down with a thunk on the side table.

"Besotted? She only arrived a few hours before you did."

Theo nodded wisely. "So you're saying you need more time to fall firmly into her clutches. I understand."

"You and Viola are a terrible pair." Drew glared at his brother. "I'd thank you to stop pushing Me—Miss Clarke at me. I'm not marrying anyone, at least not immediately."

"Thus disappointing all the mamas of the *ton*. At least with you as the most eligible bachelor in the room, they're not casting their nets —or their daughters—at me."

"So you're content with your lowly viscountancy after all?" Drew couldn't resist the dig.

Theo let out a theatrical sigh. "I suppose I must be, since you won't remove the burden from my bent shoulders."

"Scapegrace."

"Snob."

They solemnly clinked their brandy glasses together, then starting laughing at the same moment.

"I'm glad you're here," Drew said. "Even if you insist on being a thorn in my side."

"Someone must." His brother grinned at him. "Let's go see if the tree has toppled over yet."

CHAPTER 7

*L*uncheon was a stilted affair. Mena did her best to aid the conversation, which Lady Viola valiantly carried along. The gentlemen did what they could, but the older ladies scarcely spoke a word, let alone acknowledged one another's presence. Directly after the meal the duchess excused herself, claiming she must meet with the housekeeper. Mena's mother went the opposite direction, back to her suite.

"It's snowing again," Lady Viola said, glancing at the darkening windows as the rest of the party left the dining room. "So much for sleigh rides."

"We'll go out tomorrow," the duke said. "Surely we can find some other amusements to occupy the afternoon."

"Carol singing?" his brother suggested.

Lady Viola shook her head. "Not until Mother's in a better mood. What about fashioning decorations for that enormous tree?"

"Too tedious," the viscount said. "I did my duty in fetching it—the rest of you can see to the adornments."

His sister cocked her head. "Last year, the Ashfords had silver-foil paper chains draping their tree, if I recall. Perhaps we can make something along similar lines. And frosted gingerbread men, of course."

"Gingerbread." The duke nodded his approval.

"You mustn't touch them," Lady Viola said, one finger lifted in admonishment. "They are for decoration, not devouring."

"Remember the ginger cake Cook's former assistant used to make?" Viscount Thornton asked.

"Parkin cake," the duke said, and Mena shot him a surprised look. "That was the best flavor of the holidays, without question. A pity the assistant's gone."

His sister nodded. "Nobody else can make it properly."

The corner of Mena's mouth twitched as the beginnings of a plan hatched in her mind.

"Miss Clarke, you look like the cat that ate the canary," the duke said. "Go on, spit it out."

She wasn't going to reveal her thoughts that easily. Instead, she scrambled for a response. Luckily, their surroundings provided one.

"Perhaps we should have a race down the hallway." She gestured at the length of the corridor. "For old times' sake."

"Ha!" The viscount shook out his cuffs. "I accept the challenge."

"As do I!" Lady Viola took up her skirts in both hands and grinned at Mena.

The duke looked at her, a spark of mirth in his eyes. "Very well. I'll let you win, as usual."

She pivoted toward him, hands on her hips. "You never did! I earned my victories fair and square."

"You know she's right," Lady Viola said to her brother. "For I had to listen to you complain afterward. Ready? On the count of three…"

The moment Lady Viola spoke the final number, Mena was off. She heard Viola laughing behind her, the viscount exclaiming in annoyance, and the muffled thud of the duke's steps matching her own. Drawing on all her frustration and worry, she forced her legs to move faster beneath her swishing skirts. It was like old times, except that the disapproving portraits on the wall flashed by at shoulder height instead of frowning above her head.

Almost there. Her corset squeezed her lungs, and her breath emerged in short gasps, but she refused to stop. Not before she won, at any rate.

"Aiee!" Mrs. Simmons rounded the corner, directly into Mena's path. The housekeeper threw up her arms, spilling the basket of candles she was carrying.

Mena tried to stop from careening into the woman, but she was going too fast. The crash was inevitable—

And then strong hands caught her by the shoulders, pulling her to a stop. She bumped back against the tall, solid length of the Duke of Beckford, whose chest was also rising and falling, though not as rapidly as her own.

"Your pardon," he said to Mrs. Simmons, who had begun sputtering with indignation. "Miss Clarke thought she saw a, er—"

"A large spider," Mena supplied hastily. "I'm afraid I have quite an aversion, and took to my heels."

The housekeeper gave her an offended look. "Dovington Hall is free of any pests, I assure you."

"Except for the moths," Lady Viola said, accompanying her brother down the hall at a decorous pace, though her cheeks were tellingly flushed. "And the little family of mice in the lavender sitting room, and the—"

"Enough," the duke said. "We're certainly not faulting your standards, Mrs. Simmons. I'm certain everything is as it should be."

"Well," the housekeeper said, and bent to gather the spilled tapers. "If you say so, Your Grace."

With a reproving look, she took up her basket and then stalked past them.

"I suppose we shouldn't try sliding down the banisters," the viscount said once she'd disappeared into the dining room. "Then we'd be in trouble, indeed."

"A pity," the duke said, his voice vibrating through Mena.

Belatedly she realized she was still leaning against him in a most untoward manner. She took a quick step away, hoping the warmth of exertion on her face hid her blush.

"Thank you, Your Grace," she said, then shook out her skirts, still slightly askew from their race.

Not so easily shaken off, however, was the memory of his warmth at her back.

"My pleasure," he said. "I consider it my duty to prevent calamitous collisions in the halls of my home, whenever possible."

"Miss Clarke still won," Lady Viola said.

"Whether you kept her from running over Mrs. Simmons or not."

"We'll call it draw," Mena said, still a trifle unbalanced. When the duke raised a brow at her, she gave him a tight smile in return. "I'm just trying to protect my teacakes, you understand."

"Your teacakes?" Lady Viola asked.

"As I recall," Mena said, "your brother used to steal them from my plate as forfeits for his losses. Unjustified, I might add."

The duke threw his head back and laughed, and Mena tried not to stare at the strong line of his jaw and throat. Heavens, he'd become distractingly handsome. Though no less annoying, she told herself firmly.

"I'd all but forgotten," he said.

His sister shook her head at him. "You and your fondness for cake."

"It's my only weakness," he said. "I'm an exemplary fellow in all other ways."

"It will be your downfall one day," the viscount said, waggling his brows.

"Most unlikely." The duke prodded his brother with an elbow. "What do you propose we do next, if not slide down the banisters?"

"How about a hand or two of whist?"

"An excellent plan." Lady Viola looped her

arm through Mena's. "I claim Miss Clarke as my partner."

"I must warn you," Mena said as Lady Viola towed her along, "I'm not particularly skilled at cards." Indeed, the last time she recalled touching a deck was under that very same roof, when they used to play hand after hand of Old Maid.

Curious how the longer she spent at Dovington Hall, the more memories emerged. Had anyone asked her even a week ago if she'd spent much time in her childhood with the Duke of Beckford's family, she would have said no. But now recollections clustered, thick as the winter shadows, in every corner of the grand estate.

Perhaps the painful falling-out between their mothers had caused her to lock those memories away into a heavy iron-bound trunk. Now, however, the lid had cracked open, and Mena wasn't sure what to think. Especially when it came to the current duke.

Were they truly at odds—or had they been close companions all along?

"Never fear," Lady Viola said. "Both of my brothers are dreadful players. Why do you suppose I chose you?"

"In that case, I can't possibly refuse," Mena

said, resolving to stop fretting about the past. And the duke.

Hazel eyes sparkling with amusement, Lady Viola led them to Dovington Hall's billiards room. A Turkish rug patterned in red and blue covered the floor, spreading beneath the felt-covered table in the center of the room. Two ornate chandeliers hung from the ceiling, and a fire burned in the hearth beneath an enormous painting depicting fields and rolling hills at sunrise.

"I'll deal," Viscount Thornton said, snagging an inlaid card box from the wooden shelves on the far wall.

"Don't you trust me?" his sister said sweetly as she went to the table set closest to the mullioned windows.

"Not particularly."

"Miss Clarke, allow me," the duke said, pulling out a chair for her, then doing the same for his sister once Mena had settled.

The gentlemen took their places on either side, the viscount shuffled the cards, and they commenced playing.

As promised, Lady Viola was quite the cutthroat player, guiding Mena through the subtleties of whist as they defeated the gentlemen three games in a row. Snow drifted lazily down outside the windows, but the fire on the hearth kept the room cozy. It was warmed further still by the gentle ribbing between the siblings, the laughter and camaraderie folding about Mena like a soft wool blanket.

At last the viscount shut his cards with a snap and pushed away from the table.

"That's enough punishment for one day," he said. "I concede."

"You can't just give in," the duke said sternly.

"Oh, but of a surety, I can." Lord Thornton stood and made them an ostentatious bow. "I know when to beat a graceful retreat. Bonjour, ladies, by your leave."

"It's hardly graceful if you mention how graceful you are," Lady Viola said tartly. "But go on, the both of you. Miss Clarke and I have things to discuss."

They did? Mena raised her brows at Lady Viola, and received a conspiratorial smile in return.

"That's not ominous in the least," Lord Beckford said, standing. "Pray, don't get up to more mischief than Dovington Hall can contain."

He inclined his head to Mena, shot his sister a warning look, and accompanied Viscount Thornton from the room.

As soon as the gentlemen were gone, Lady Viola leaned forward.

"If Christmas is going to be any fun at all," she said, "we must find a way to mend things between your mother and mine."

"Yes." Mena pushed at the edge of the card deck, straightening the pile with her thumb. "But I've no notion how. Neither of them will apologize."

"There must be a way. Perhaps if we locked them in one of the parlors until they started speaking..."

"It would take years," Mena said. "I think our only hope is that they begin to recall their friendship."

Just as she had, the memories descending as surely as the snowflakes flurrying outside.

"I hope so." Lady Viola looked pensive for a moment. "What do you know of their falling out? There might be a clue there as to how we might set things to rights."

Mena stopped poking at the cards, and folded her hands in her lap. "According to my parents, your mother had loaned mine a sapphire necklace, which became misplaced. There were...accusations." She cleared her throat. "I don't like to speak of it."

"My mother implied it was not an accidental loss," Lady Viola said. "Yes, I know—that was unconscionably rude. But I believe my father was the instigator. He didn't approve of their friendship."

Mena gave her a sharp look. "Why not?"

"He was of an older generation that, quite frankly, was far too conscious of its own social status."

A pang went through Mena. "You're saying that since my mother was of common blood, the old duke didn't want her to associate with his wife. Even though my mother married a member of the nobility."

Minor nobility—which evidently wasn't good enough for Lord Beckford's family. The knowledge stung, and she rose from her chair to stare blindly at the snow swirling outside.

"I know what you're thinking." Lady Viola held out her hand. "But please, don't leave. We want you here."

"Your mother doesn't." Mena gripped the back of her chair.

The polished wood was unyielding under her fingers—as hard as the knowledge that her father's choice of a wife had cast shadows that reached across their entire family history. And future.

"My mother is only upset because yours never replied to her apology," Lady Viola said.

"Apology?" Mena blinked at her. "I don't believe one was ever offered."

Brows rising, Lady Viola stood to face her. "I'm quite certain the duchess tendered at least one very heartfelt letter. But…"

"What if it never reached its destination?" Mena finished for her.

They stood for a moment, staring at one another. Mena's heart ached for the misery her mother had endured, all the more bitter if it had been deliberately caused.

"We must find those letters," Lady Viola said with a determined expression.

"If they still exist." Hope was like a newly lit candle in Mena's chest. She didn't know whether to cup her hand around the fresh flame to coax it along, or blow it out altogether for fear of it burning her.

"If they don't," Lady Viola said, "then our mothers simply must speak—and believe one another's words."

A task easier said than done. "Where do you think such letters might be?"

"I'll ask Drew if he came across any unopened correspondence when he inherited—though I must think he would've mentioned such a thing. Perhaps they're hidden in the library somewhere."

Hidden in the library. Or…her father's study. A sense of betrayal rose in Mena, tingling up from the soles of her feet.

But no, surely not.

Still, she couldn't be easy until she'd returned to Marston Mews and searched the hidden compartment in her father's desk. A compartment she'd glimpsed once, nearly ten years prior, when she'd delivered tea to his study.

"Mena." He'd stuffed some papers into a small drawer she didn't recall ever seeing before, and rose to take the tea tray from her. "Kind of you to bring my tea, but do knock next time."

She *had* bumped the door with her foot, as her hands had been occupied with bearing the tray, but clearly he hadn't heard her.

"Of course, Father. Enjoy your tea."

She hadn't thought much of it, until that moment. But perhaps Lady Viola's father wasn't the only one who'd colluded to keep the families apart.

CHAPTER 8

Drew pulled his top hat lower over his forehead, shading his eyes from the brilliant, icy sparkles as he guided the sleigh over the new snow. The runners made a shushing noise as the horse pulled the sleigh briskly down the fir-lined drive—nearly the only sound in the muffled landscape he and Mena traveled through.

Well, that and the ring of Viola and Theo's voices drifting back from the front sleigh as they argued about decorating the tree.

The morning had dawned clear and full of promise. After breakfast—marked by both his mother's and Lady Marston's absence—the rest of them had decided to go sleighing down to the village. At the appointed hour, he, Theo, Viola, and Mena gathered by the front door.

"I'm glad to see you found your hat," Mena

said to him as they stepped outside into the cold morning air, where the grooms had the horse-drawn sleighs waiting.

"If not my decorum?" He grinned at her. "Your bonnet is fetching, Miss Clarke."

Or perhaps it was the face beneath it that he found of such interest, despite the suspicious look in her brown eyes.

"It isn't, particularly," she said. "Not like my favorite hat—which I'll have you know was ruined by the snow, after all."

"I'm sorry to hear it," he said, neglecting to mention that the maids had brought word to the housekeeper right away, as he'd asked, and the matter was being seen to.

As the party descended the front steps, the matched grays tossed their heads in the traces, a little confused to be separated and put to work pulling these odd contraptions instead of the usual carriage. They were good steeds, though, and Drew knew they'd settle as soon as the party set off.

"I'll ride with Theo," Viola said, setting her hand on the curved edge of the front sleigh and giving Drew a significant look. "You and Miss Clarke drive together. Shall we stop at the inn for luncheon?"

"I recall they make a fine steak-and-ale pie," Theo said, nodding. "I approve this plan."

"Is that agreeable to you, Miss Clarke?" Drew asked, handing her into the sleigh. "My siblings tend to be somewhat high-handed."

"Your entire family is horribly opinionated," she said, her smile taking the sting from her words. "But if I objected, I assure you I'd speak my mind."

"I'm relieved to hear it." He settled beside her and took up the reins, trying not to pay any heed to the warmth of her against his side. "Sometimes, I've found, people are afraid to voice their objections to a duke."

She arched one brow. "It's hard to be over-awed by a boy I once shoved into the pond."

"Ha!" He couldn't help his burst of laughter. "As I recall, I pushed you in first."

"Only up to my ankles," she replied. "You, however, were soaked to the skin."

"And got a thorough scolding from my tutor, I'll have you know."

"Didn't you tell him you were studying amphibians?" she asked innocently.

"He was unsympathetic." Drew grinned at her. "Do you know, I'd nearly forgotten how much time we used to spend roaming the estate. I'm sorry our parents had a falling out."

"I am, too." She dropped her gaze and busied herself with tucking the fur-lined lap robe more securely about her legs. "But you were off to Eton, at any rate."

"Still, I missed seeing you at the holidays—at least for the first few years." He didn't realize how true the words were, until he spoke them.

"I think, when we're younger, we learn not to pine for things we can't have." She gazed pensively over the white landscape.

"And now?" He briefly laid his gloved hand over hers.

She looked back at him, unsmiling. "Now, life continues as it may."

"What will you do when you reach London?"

"Find lodging, and then employment." She pulled her hand from beneath his.

Viola had hinted as much, but Mena's words shocked him. He wanted to ask what her father had been thinking, to leave his family in such straits—but despite their growing friendship, he was reluctant to dig into such a clearly painful subject.

"Your silence speaks volumes," she said dryly, after the silence had stretched overlong. "Are you embarrassed to be seen with a woman of such few means that she must become a governess?"

"Not in the least," he said stoutly, hoping it was true.

"Well, that's a departure from your familial norm."

He frowned at her. "We're not all like my mother. If that were so, you wouldn't be here beside me, nor Lady Marston enjoying the comforts of the Ivory Suite."

"Stop the sleigh." She flung the robe off her lap and began to rise. "Next you'll be telling me how grateful we should be for your scraps of generosity and, quite frankly, Your Grace, I'd rather walk back to Dovington in the snow than endure your superior airs."

He reached out to steady her. "Miss Clarke, please sit. I'm sorry if I've offended—"

The rest of his apology went unspoken as the sleigh hit a bump. Mena lost her footing and would've tumbled from the vehicle, but Drew snatched her about the waist and pulled her back. She sprawled awkwardly across his lap as he pulled the horse to a halt one-handed, his pulse racing. For a moment all he could think of was the feel of her against him, her face upturned to his in surprise.

Their breath frosted together in the air as their gazes held for a long moment. His heart-beat thumped in the snow-hushed quiet and he dipped his head, their lips almost brushing...

Then she pushed away from him, color

rising in her cheeks, and he was abruptly returned to his senses.

"My apologies," he said, then cleared his throat. "Please, Mena, don't walk back. I'll turn the sleigh around and drive you, if that's what you want."

Lips pressed together, she shook her head. Something flashed in her eyes, and he hoped she wouldn't accuse him of snobbery once again. Even if—though he hated to admit it—there might be some truth to her words.

Ahead of them, Theo and Viola had finally noticed that the second sleigh had stopped.

"Is everything well?" Theo called, slowing his vehicle.

"One moment," Drew called back, then glanced at Mena.

"We can continue to the village," she said stiffly. "However, there is something you might do to make amends."

"I'd be delighted, whatever it is." He waved to Theo to drive on, then clucked the horse back into motion. Their sleigh glided serenely forward, in direct contrast to the jumble of his thoughts.

"Well, then." Mena tucked the lap robe over their knees once more. "I require you to pay a call upon the new Baron Marston this very afternoon."

"You do?" He blinked at the unexpected request.

"After we finish luncheon at the inn, we can continue over to Marston Mews," she went on, as though he hadn't spoken.

"We must send word to Lord Marston, at least." A duke didn't go about making unannounced visits, after all. It would be an inconvenience at best, to arrive at the baron's doorstep without warning.

Her mouth twitched with impatience. "Then send one of the village lads to Marston Mews while we take our meal."

"My siblings will accompany us," he reminded her. It would be most improper for the two of them to go alone.

Especially after what had just transpired. Had he truly almost kissed Mena?

"Of course," she said. "Indeed, perhaps I'll ride with Viola. I presume she knows how to drive a sleigh, and if she does not, I'll manage."

"Unnecessary. If I'm to pay this impromptu call, then you will ride with me. Dare I ask why this visit is required?"

"Don't you want to welcome the new baron to Yorkshire?" she asked archly. "Or is he too far beneath your notice?"

He kept his expression smooth. "I was

thinking he might come pay his regards to *me*, as is far more customary."

"Well, now he won't need to." She sent him an insincere smile.

"Why this sudden solicitude for the new baron? After all, he threw you and your mother out into the snow mere days before Christmas. I find it curious that you want to make sure he's welcomed into the neighborhood."

She glanced away, and he had the sudden suspicion there was more to the matter than met the eye.

"Perhaps I'd like to see Marston Mews and the staff once more before I leave Yorkshire," she said.

"Perhaps." He didn't quite believe her, but they were sweeping down into the village and the time for questions was over. At least until after lunch.

THE INTERIOR of the Pint and Plough smelled of peat smoke and ale. The few patrons at the bar made their respectful greetings to the duke and his party as the innkeeper hurried over to show them to a table. Mena glanced about with a pang, suddenly realizing this would be the last time she set foot in the cozy pub.

Not that they'd frequented it regularly, but she and her family had enjoyed their share of meals in the half-timbered room over the years.

"We won't be heading back to Dovington Hall right away," the duke told his siblings as they settled into a nook table tucked beside one of the many-paned windows. "Miss Clarke has requested a detour to Marston Mews."

"Indeed?" His brother shot him a curious glance. "That seems...a touch precipitous."

"I've sent a lad to inform Lord Marston of our plans," the duke said, without further explanation.

Indeed, the moment he and Mena had disembarked from the sleigh, he'd pressed a coin into one of the stable boy's hands and instructed him to make haste to Marston Mews and inform the baron that Lord Beckford would be calling upon him that same afternoon.

Lady Viola slanted a look at Mena, questions in her eyes, but seemed willing to hold her patience, and her tongue. The innkeeper brought cider and his trademark pies to the table, and for a time they busied themselves with lunch.

Mena ate her steak-and-ale pie and praised its flavor, but in truth she barely tasted her food. Her mind was occupied with a whirl of emotion. The shocking moment when Drew had almost kissed her danced a merry jig with her apprehension about the upcoming visit to Marston Mews, the thoughts spinning about her head until she felt rather dizzy.

Surely she'd misconstrued that moment when she'd so embarrassingly landed in Drew's lap. After all, if even Mr. Whittaker didn't want her, why would a duke? No, it must have been a passing fancy. Or nothing at all.

Whatever the case, she needed to stop thinking about Drew, and work out how she might slip away to the study at Marston Mews to search for hidden letters. If there were any there to be found, that was. Her memory might be faulty, or her father might have long ago disposed of the correspondence she thought she'd glimpsed, or the new baron tossed them into the fire, or—Really, there were any number of reasons she shouldn't be planning to illicitly search her father's old desk.

And yet, if those letters existed, she must uncover them.

As they finished their meal, Mena caught Lady Viola's eye and nodded to the powder room tucked beneath the stairs. The duke's sister took her meaning immediately.

"Mena and I going to freshen up," Viola said, standing. "We'll meet you outside."

As soon as they reached the privacy of the small washroom, Viola turned to Mena, questions sparkling in her eyes.

"I need your help," Mena said, without preamble. "I'm going to search the study at Marston Mews."

"How excitingly covert! I suppose I can provide a suitable distraction, if necessary. Do you think you'll find anything?"

"I don't know." Mena wasn't certain whether she wanted to or not, when it came down to it.

Proof that her father had colluded to keep the families apart would be extremely distressing, especially to her mother. With a sigh, she turned to the tarnished mirror to re-pin her hair, which had become slightly disheveled during the first portion of the sleigh ride.

"I'll assist you however I can," Viola said, adjusting her hat. "And I must admit, I'm quite curious to meet the new baron and his family. No doubt it will be an illuminating visit."

CHAPTER 9

As the sleigh drew up outside Marston Mews, Mena found herself gripping the edge of the lap robe quite tightly. She let out a breath and forced her fingers to relax, then patted the crushed fur back into place as best she could.

The duke disembarked and handed the reins to Tommy, who was standing outside, clearly awaiting their arrival. Mena sent him a quick smile, and the boy ducked his head shyly in return.

Lord Beckford rounded the sleigh and offered his hand.

"Are you well, Miss Clarke?" he asked, giving her a concerned look as she stepped from the vehicle.

"Quite," she said, lifting her chin, though his perceptiveness annoyed her.

She didn't need Lord Beckford looking at her with those sympathetic hazel-flecked eyes. It made her feel vulnerable, and a little afraid— and she most emphatically wanted to be neither of those things as she set foot for the last time in her childhood home.

Lady Viola and Lord Thornton came up behind them, and Viola gave Mena's shoulder a brief pat of reassurance as they reached the doorstep.

The door opened, revealing a harried-looking Mrs. Taff. Behind her, the sound of shrill voices increased in volume, accompanied by the clatter of running feet.

"Brace yourselves," Mena murmured.

A mob of children spilled out of the house, parted like a rushing stream about the visitors, and scattered into the snow-filled yard. The nurse and governess pursued them, brandishing coats, hats, and mufflers.

"Children," screeched the governess, who, as Mena recalled, was the new baron's aunt.

The baron's offspring paid her no mind and gleefully began throwing handfuls of snow at one another. The governess paused on the stoop and shot a startled glance at the duke and his party, her eyes widening.

"Your Grace," she said, dropping a hurried curtsey, then scrambled after her charges.

The duke tipped his hat as she went past. "A pleasure, I'm sure."

"Please come in, Your Grace." Mrs. Taff curtsied and beckoned them forward. "Lord Marston and his family are awaiting you in the parlor."

"Certainly." Lord Beckford stepped through the doorway, followed by Mena, Lady Viola, and Lord Thornton, who looked like he'd rather be out flinging snow with the children than paying this particular social call.

As they went down the hall, Mena glanced about. Already, Marston Mews seemed changed. The table beside the door had switched places with the umbrella stand, the strong scent of lemon assaulted her nose, and a rag doll lay abandoned at the foot of the stairs. There was no mistaking that the house belonged to Cousin Basil's family now.

The new Lord Marston met them at the parlor door. He greeted the duke effusively, then showed the party in, introduced his wife and her parents, and invited everyone to sit.

"Such an honor, Your Grace," Lady Marston said, her tone slightly smug. "Just imagine, you paying a call on *us*."

The duke shot Mena the flicker of a glance, one brow twitching up. She knew she deserved the gentle rebuke—but she'd had good reason to bend the social norms. She hoped.

"We were in the village," Drew said to their hostess. "It seemed reasonable that we stop by and welcome you to the neighborhood."

"And a fine neighborhood it is," Lord Marston said. "We look forward to attending the parties you no doubt throw at Dovington Hall."

An awkward silence followed his words, and Mena felt a twist of shame. These were her relatives, no matter how distant, and the new baron had all but invited himself to Dovington.

"Indeed," Lady Viola said brightly. "We have nothing in the offing this season, but rest assured that at some point we'd be delighted to host an event for the entire neighborhood."

The duke nodded, looking relieved, while Lord Thornton coughed lightly into his sleeve.

"Ah, here comes Mrs. Taff with tea and refreshments," the baroness said, waving the housekeeper to come in.

Mrs. Taff entered, pushing the tea trolley, which she deposited next to the baroness. Mena saw that they had at least brought out she best silver tea service and china in honor of their guests.

"Is that parkin cake?" the duke asked, leaning forward to inspect the tray of sweets.

"It is," Lady Marston said. "And lemon tarts, as well."

"Have a tart," the baron said. "Sadly, the cook seems to have mislaid her parkin recipe. Though the first batch we had when we arrived was remarkably good, her current efforts are merely passable."

Mena frowned at the criticism of Mrs. Stewart's cooking, though she knew she herself was to blame for the change in the quality of the gingerbread.

After a quarter hour of slightly awkward conversation and polite tea drinking, Mena set her cup down.

"Begging your pardon," she said. "I would like to go pay my regards to Mrs. Stewart. With your permission?"

"That seems a bit familiar," the baroness's mother said in a quavering voice. "Deserting us for the servants? I wouldn't have thought—"

"I spent a fair amount of my childhood in the kitchen," Mena said, then winced at how her words sounded.

Lady Marston gave her a cold look, but the duke laughed.

"I, too, was forever hanging about the cooks at Dovington," he said. "I come honestly by my sweet tooth, I must admit. But tell me, Lord Marston, do you have plans for cultivating your new estate? I understand you've an excellent background with the land."

He'd struck just the right tone of convivial interest without giving offense, and the knot of Mena's anxiety eased. She sent an inquiring look at the baroness, who, with pinched lips, nodded her permission.

Mena stood, curtsied to the room in general, and hurried away. Once outside the parlor, she hesitated a moment to ensure no one was following her. Then, instead of turning toward the kitchen, she quickly made for the study down the hall. She would go say hello to Mrs. Stewart, of course...but not before making her search.

She reached the study door and grasped the handle, but the latch refused to give way. To her dismay, the study door was locked. Her father had never locked it—but then again, he hadn't had six children underfoot.

Frowning, Mena pulled a hairpin free and set about jiggling it in the keyhole. Luckily, it wasn't the first time she'd picked open a lock at Marston Mews, and all the doors were similar. But it took precious time she couldn't afford.

Finally, after what felt like a ticking eternity but was probably under two minutes, she heard a click as the latch released. Letting out a breath of relief, she stuck her hairpin back in her coiffure and slipped into Baron Marston's study.

Memories assailed her as she inhaled the scent of leather and furniture polish. For a moment she half expected to see her father seated behind the desk in the corner, and grief twisted in her belly. Whatever his faults, the former Baron Marston had tried to do his best for his family.

And she was there to discover what, precisely, some of those efforts had been.

Mauve skirts swishing, she went to the desk. If she recalled correctly, the secret drawer had been located on the left-hand side—a thin wedge, concealed by the upper drawer's paneling. She pulled the top drawer open and felt about the outer sides and bottom, with no result.

Very well—the catch must be inside the drawer somewhere. Carefully, she lifted out a leather-bound folio and several loose sheets of paper and set them on the desk, then resumed her exploration.

Finally, her fingernail encountered a protrusion in the front center of the drawer. Could that be it? Biting her lip, Mena pressed upon it.

Without a sound, the secret drawer slid open a quarter inch. She pulled it open, her heart pounding so loudly that she feared the whole room echoed with the thudding inside her chest.

There.

A letter addressed to her mother lay atop two folded sheets of paper. Mena didn't know whether to be relieved or entirely dismayed to discover this proof of her father's perfidy.

"Miss Clarke?" The new baroness's voice echoed down the hallway.

Mena snatched up the letters and slammed the drawers shut, hoping the secret opening would close itself snugly without her assistance.

"Miss Clarke?" The study door opened to reveal her hostess. Lady Marston looked her up and down, suspicion bright in her eyes. "Whatever are you doing in here?"

"Ah…" Mena thought furiously. "I was looking for a sheet of paper and a pencil, you see." She waved the blank side of the papers at Lady Marston, then grabbed the stub of a pencil from the desk and shoved everything into the pocket of her skirts. "I must confess, I've been keeping a secret."

"That seems quite clear." The baroness frowned at her, affronted. "I insist you reveal it at once."

"It concerns the cook," Mena said, rounding the desk. "And if you'd care to come with me to the kitchen, you may see for yourself."

Despite her indignation, it seemed Lady Marston's interest was piqued. She gave a tight nod as Mena sidled past, then stalked like an angry starling at Mena's back as she headed for the kitchen.

"Miss Mena!" Mrs. Stewart said, wiping her hands on her apron and smiling broadly as Mena stepped through the door. Her smile fell when she saw the baroness at Mena's heels.

"Mrs. Stewart," Mena said, holding herself back from rushing to embrace the cook. "It's good to see you."

"Dispense with the pleasantries, Miss Clarke," Lady Marston said coldly, "and explain."

Mena drew in a breath and turned to her hostess. "I must tell you that...Well, the fact of the matter is that Mrs. Stewart didn't *lose* the parkin cake recipe. She never had it to begin with. I'm the one who baked the gingerbread for your arrival."

"You?" Lady Marston sounded surprised.

"Yes." Mena rubbed her fingers against her skirts. "It's my grandmother's recipe. I must admit that I didn't share it with Mrs. Stewart, though she asked me to."

Lady Marston's lips firmed into a thin line as she glanced from Mena to the cook.

"That explains a few things," the baroness said. "But not everything, Miss Clarke—such as why I found you rummaging about in the study."

"I was sorry for my lack of generosity," Mena said. "After your husband mentioned how much he'd enjoyed the parkin, my conscience could no longer allow me to withhold the recipe from Mrs. Stewart. In the spirit of the holidays, I decided to share it with her, which is why I was in the study, looking for something to write the recipe down upon."

"Miss Mena, how kind!" Mrs. Stewart said, shifting slightly to conceal her receipt box, which, in addition to her tried-and-true recipes, held blank cards and a stick of graphite. "I've asked you so many times to share your family recipe."

Mena managed a smile. "Well, now I shall. The trick is to begin with boiled milk, you see, into which you slowly stir the treacle—"

"Very good," Lady Marston said. "Write it down, Miss Clarke, and rejoin us in the parlor. I trust you can find your way without becoming lost in the other rooms?"

"Of course, Lady Marston." Mena dipped the baroness a shallow curtsey, though their relative stations didn't require it. Still, it was best to flatter the woman's vanity.

"I expect to see you posthaste." Lady Marston gave her one last, steely look, then turned on her heel and headed out of the kitchen.

As soon as she was gone, Mena blew out a long breath.

"And what was all that about, miss?" Mrs. Stewart asked, going to her receipt box and plucking out a blank card.

"A personal matter," Mena replied. "But truly, I was also planning to give you the parkin cake recipe."

She bent over the scarred wooden kitchen table and began to write the instructions, trying to keep her hand steady as her eyes filled with moisture. This was the last time she'd stand in the warmth of Marston Mews' kitchen, and the finality of it struck her to the core.

When she'd finished, she handed the card to Mrs. Stewart, who enfolded her in an embrace.

"Thank you, dearie," the cook said. "My, but I'm going to miss you."

Mena nodded, blotting her tears with the back of her sleeve. "Take good care of yourself, Mrs. Stewart. And enjoy the parkin."

The cook pressed her hand. "Every time I make it, I'll think of you."

Mena nodded and stepped out of the kitchen, then paused to take several deep breaths. She must collect herself. It wouldn't do to return to the parlor with sorrow shining in her eyes.

The papers in her pocket felt like lead weights, but she couldn't risk looking at them in the hallway, either.

No, whatever secrets those hidden letters contained, they would have to wait until she was safely back at Dovington Hall.

CHAPTER 10

*A*s he handed Miss Clarke back into the sleigh, Drew couldn't help noticing her subdued manner. Once they were on the main road with Marston Mews receding behind them, he looked over at her.

"Is everything well?" he asked. "I can't imagine it was easy, seeing your former home occupied by another family."

"That wasn't so bad," she said. "The place is lively, at any rate."

"To say the least. Though I'd hope one becomes accustomed to the clamor of children after a time."

"You'd have to ask your mother about that," she said. "Certainly she can speak to the experience."

He raised his brows in mock offense. "We were model offspring, I assure you."

"Mm. Like the time you and Theo set a half-dozen frogs loose on the dining room table?" She tilted her head. "Or the chimney expedition of 1840? As I recall, we emerged covered in soot from head to toe, and tracked ashes all over the carpets."

"Grand times." He smiled to see her mood lifting. "Is it true you know how to bake the best parkin cake in the land?"

"I do, yes."

"And not modest about it, either."

Her mouth twitched. "No need to be modest about the truth, Your Grace."

"I prefer Your Most Eminent Grace, in casual conversation," he said, trying—and failing—to keep the laughter from his voice.

"Really, Drew, you make the most peculiar duke," she said. Then her gloved hand flew up to cover her mouth and she gave him a wide-eyed look. "Begging your pardon for the familiarity."

"I'll tolerate it," he said, something vibrating through him he couldn't quite name. "If you'll allow me to call you Mena from time to time."

Her cheeks were already flushed from the cold, but he fancied they grew a touch redder.

"That's rather forward of you, sir."

Not nearly as forward as his thoughts. He rather desperately wanted to lean over, fold her into his arms, and let his mouth graze hers, fulfilling the promise of their earlier almost-kiss. If the unattended horse ran them into a snowbank, he wouldn't care.

As long as he could kiss Mena.

But would she welcome his attentions? She'd already pushed him away once.

He gave an inward sigh and steered the conversation, and the sleigh, onto safer ground.

"I confess I'd like to try this famous parkin of yours," he said. "The baron couldn't keep from extolling its virtues. It was kind of you to pass the details along to the cook."

Lady Marston had made no qualms about divulging what Mena was doing in the kitchen —possibly to boast to her husband that they were now in possession of the coveted parkin cake recipe, and possibly to cut down Mena's status by implying that she was overly familiar with the household staff.

"It was the least I could do. A parting gift." Mena blew out a breath, a plume of white in the air, and turned her head to watch the frosty landscape pass.

He focused on guiding the sleigh through the village, steering around a stray chicken that seemed quite confused by the snow, and waving at two boys who whooped at the sleigh as they flew past.

From behind them came Theo's answering call, and Viola's laugh.

"Are you warm enough?" Drew asked after they'd left the last stone-walled houses behind.

"Quite," Mena said. "Besides, we'll be back at Dovington Hall soon enough."

"I believe Theo has proposed a game of charades when we return," he said. "Unless you and Viola would like to soundly defeat us in whist again."

Both prospects were preferable to being roped into making the tiny silver-paper chains his sister insisted they must drape about the entire tree before tomorrow evening. Or, an equally wearying task, going over the account books that waited upon his desk.

"I'm afraid I must beg off," Mena said. "I've barely seen my mother in days, and we have… things to discuss."

He shot her a quick look. "I hope you know that the two of you are welcome to stay at Dovington as long as you'd like. Indeed, I wish you would."

The thought of them heading off to London, to dicey prospects at best, made him increasingly uncomfortable. Mena deserved better from life—and her mother did, too.

She pleated the lap robe between her gloved

fingers. "I don't think that's necessary, though I thank you for your hospitality."

"It's not an imposition."

"I know." She lifted her head, her gaze holding his. "But I believe it's best to begin the year as we mean to go on."

Penniless, and with no prospects? he wanted to ask angrily, but forced himself to swallow the words. Mena and Lady Marston were too proud to take his charity, and he couldn't force it upon them, much as he might wish to do so.

They turned off on the drive to Dovington, and Theo and Viola pulled level with them.

"Race?" his brother called.

Drew looked at Mena. "What do you think, Miss Clarke?"

She glanced at the other sleigh, then back to him. He was glad to see a spark of mischief ignite in her eyes.

"Very well," she said. "But only if we win."

"That goes without saying." He shook the reins, and they shot forward.

Theo, of course, had anticipated the move, and they whooshed neck and neck down the drive. At the turn, Drew had the advantage of the inside curve, and had to admit he didn't mind when Mena pressed up against him, clutching his arm for balance as the vehicle teetered.

Once they straightened, she didn't move away. With a gleeful grin, Drew brought them down the straightaway and into a graceful glide, halting before the front door. Theo and Viola were only a heartbeat behind them as they all piled out of the sleighs, laughing.

The entrance hall was redolent with the smell of fir, and the tree, he had to admit, looked rather majestic, even without being fully decorated. They doffed their outerwear, and Viola linked her arm with Mena's.

"Come, Miss Clarke," she said. "Show me what you plan to wear tomorrow for Christmas Eve."

"It's lavender," Mena warned. "Do recall I'm still in half mourning."

"Of course. But I found a sash this morning that might be just the thing to go with it." Viola looked at her brothers. "Go on and amuse yourselves, lads. We'll see you at dinner."

"Your Majesty." Drew sketched a bow, and Theo followed suit.

Viola sniffed and, nose in the air, led Mena away. As they mounted the stairs, Drew couldn't help looking after them with the strangest feeling he'd missed something of import. Though what it might be, he couldn't imagine.

"WELL?" Viola rounded on Mena the moment they reached the privacy of the Fern Suite. "Did you find anything?"

"Yes." Mena reached into her pocket, where the papers had all but burned a hole through her skirts. Pulling the letter and folded papers out, she stared at them in sudden trepidation. Did she truly want to know what they said?

"Come, sit," Viola said, heading for one of the chairs beside the hearth. "If the contents are truly terrible, you can throw them into the fire and none the wiser."

Mena perched on the edge of her chair, heart pounding. With effort, she kept her hands from trembling as she looked from the folded sheets of paper to the envelope addressed to her mother. Where to begin?

The papers, she decided. Carefully, she unfolded them. Her father's angular writing slanted across the pages, in what looked like a draft of his thoughts. Sentences were crossed out here and there, and a few notes were jotted sideways in the margins.

To her credit, Viola simply watched Mena, her brows raised, though her eyes burned with questions. Taking a deep breath, Mena silently began to read.

. . .

MY DEAREST MARTHA, *I know I should have shared this letter with you* ~~when it first arrived~~ *some time ago, yet I could not bring myself to do so. I know how deeply Lady Beckford's* ~~terrible unkind~~ *accusations wounded you, and I would spare you from further sorrow. Thus, although she professes her apology, I cannot trust either her or the duke not to cause similar hurt to you in the future. (note: did Lord B. urge his wife's behavior on? Must determine...)*

They are an old and noble family of the ton, and snobbery is bred into their bones. Despite the friendship between yourself and the duchess, I have seen how she treats you as lesser than herself, and how the duke seems to frown upon your acquaintance. (note: more kindness on my part is in order.)

Too, I must spare Philomena from the inevitable moment when the duke's offspring follow their parents' example and spurn her for her lowly roots. As a grown woman, you understand such behavior, but I fear her girlish heart might break beyond mending. ~~I do not like to see our daughter growing close to children so far above her station.~~

The pain that Lord and Lady Beckford have caused—and have the further potential to cause—has made me hesitate to show you this ~~potentially~~

~~false~~ apology for many long months. As your husband, it is my duty to protect my family from harm.

Please forgive me, my darling Martha. Eventually, I will give you this letter, but for now I feel the wounds are too fresh. I cannot, in good conscience, allow you further distress...

THROAT DRY, Mena stared at the page, trying to absorb her father's unfinished—and undelivered—words.

"Should I ring for tea?" Lady Viola asked quietly.

"Yes." Mena blinked down at the jagged writing that held so many answers, and such heartbreak. "Please."

As Viola went to the bell pull, Mena set down her father's pages and slid the letter out of its envelope. It was, indeed, an apology from Lady Beckford to her mother, filled with heartfelt sincerity and self-recrimination for her unkind behavior. In the final paragraph, the duchess had begged Mena's mother to forgive her.

That plea had gone unanswered.

Mena had to admit that the lack of response had certainly signaled that Lady Marston would not, in fact, forgive Lady Beckford. The duchess had no way of knowing that her intended recipient had never received that letter.

How shameful it must have felt, to pen such an earnest, soul-baring apology and receive no reply. No wonder she had not tried again, and hardened her heart against further interactions with her former friend.

Lady Viola settled back in her chair, watching Mena.

Slowly, Mena picked up her father's unfinished letter and ran her fingers over the creased paper.

"This is…" She cleared her throat, then looked at Viola. "It's a note penned by my father, to my mother. I don't think she ever saw it. It explains why he never gave her this."

She held up the envelope addressed to Lady Marston.

"That's the Beckford crest," Viola said. "What does it say?"

"It is the answer to the rift between our families." Mena weighed the heavy cream-colored paper in her hand. It was surprisingly light, for the burden of trouble it had caused.

"Mena." Viola leaned forward and set one hand on Mena's arm. "Whatever happened in the past, we will still be friends. I promise."

Perhaps. And perhaps not. Silently, Mena

handed Viola the letter, followed by Lord Marston's pages.

As Viola read her mother's words, her eyes widened. After going over the letter, she scanned the contents of the papers, then finally looked at Mena with a stricken expression.

"How sad," she said.

"A simple tragedy, yes." Mena wanted to feel angry, to rail against her father—and yet she understood his reasons. Perhaps a little too well.

"We shall remedy it," Viola said, voice strong with conviction. "Our mothers must read these, and then they'll understand, and be friends once again."

"Restoring their amity won't be as simple as all that," Mena said. "Their grudge has been steeping into bitterness for ten long years."

And the underlying problems still remained. If anything, the duchess had become even more entrenched within her social status. And, sadly, her son as well. Mena's heart twisted at the chasm that lay between them.

"But this changes so much about their history." Viola waved the papers at Mena.

"What if it doesn't? Perhaps it's better to leave things as they are. After all, my mother and I will be departing Yorkshire very soon." And never coming back.

"But surely we'll see you in London," Viola said.

"Where my father's fears can all come true, as Lady Beckford snubs the penniless former Baroness Marston, whose daughter has gone into service as a governess." Mena could not keep the acrimony from her voice. "No—I think it's best we leave well enough alone."

Her father's choice could stand.

"But—" Viola's words were cut off by the maid bringing in the tea, and the next several moments were spent in arranging the tea things and pouring out.

Finally, cup in hand, Lady Viola leaned back and gave Mena a penetrating look. "Are you truly going to let this injustice stand?"

"Are you going to pretend my father's concerns were without merit?" Mena replied. "We both know that, were we not in the wilds of Yorkshire, your family would never have invited mine to spend the holidays. Even if we were on amiable terms."

"You are far too unkind in your judgments." Viola set her teacup upon her saucer with an impatient clack. "My brothers both find you delightful company, as do I. Indeed, don't think I haven't seen how you and Drew look at one another."

Heat rushed into Mena's cheeks, though she

forced her voice to remain calm. "We are nothing more than old friends, reunited after many years. And once I depart Dovington Hall, we will return to being one another's distant memories."

It was the best—the only—course. No matter that Mena wished that Drew had, indeed, kissed her, or that she felt more like her true self in his company than she had for, well, a decade. There was no future that encompassed the both of them.

Viola narrowed her eyes and gave a stubborn shake of her head. "Not if I have anything to say about it."

"Well, you don't." Mena reached over and snatched back the papers tucked beside the tea tray. For a brief moment she considered doing as Viola had first suggested, and flinging them into the flames.

But no.

Despite her words to the contrary, she knew she must share the correspondence with her mother. There had been enough unhappiness and lies, and in good conscience she couldn't perpetuate them. Even if reading the letters changed nothing about their current circumstances whatsoever.

CHAPTER 11

$\mathcal{A}$fternoon light lay across his desk as Drew stared at the column of figures in the ledger open before him. In truth, he couldn't concentrate on the numbers. All he could do was think about Mena's warmth against his side as they'd raced down the drive, the challenge in her smile when she looked at him.

Her forthright manner was one of the best things about renewing their acquaintance—the steady way she regarded him without blushes or giggles, how she was unafraid to speak her mind in his presence. A pang went through him at the thought of losing that friendship again.

Once she and Lady Marston were established in London, he would seek them out, he decided. It didn't matter what the gossips might think. Or his own mother.

"Your Grace?" One of the footmen knocked at the open study door.

"Come," Drew called.

The man stepped into the room, carrying a hatbox tied up with paper and string. "The package you requested has arrived."

"Excellent—set it here, on my desk."

It had taken some doing, but with Viola's help, Drew had been able to determine the shop where Mena had procured her now-ruined hat. He'd immediately dispatched a servant with all haste to London, and hoped the man would return in time with Mena's new hat.

Which, thankfully, he had.

Drew could hardly wait to present it to her on Christmas Eve.

The trimmings likely wouldn't be the same, but he hoped the replacement would be up to snuff. In fact, he ought to look it over, with Viola's help, to make sure. Ladies' bonnets were not particularly within his area of expertise.

"Please fetch my sister," he told the footman as the servant prepared to take his leave.

"Sir," the man said, bowing.

Drew pulled the package over and began untying the string. He was just pulling the paper aside when his sister came into the study.

"Oh, it came!" she said, hurrying over to the desk. "Just in time. How does it look?"

"I haven't gotten it open yet," he said with a touch of annoyance.

"You are so slow." Pushing his hands away, she yanked off the remaining string, folded the paper back, and opened the hatbox.

Nestled inside was a blue velvet hat trimmed with ivory silk roses. It seemed very much the same as the one that had been damaged by melting snow, though the flowers were perhaps a different color.

"What do you think?" he asked his sister. "Other than admiring them perched upon ladies' heads, I haven't made a deep study of fashionable headwear. Will it suit?"

"Perfectly." Viola drew the hat out and rotated it back and forth, nodding. "I think she'll be delighted."

"I hope so. It seemed the least I could do, after dumping half her luggage into the snow."

Viola tucked the hat back into its box, then gave him a pointed look. "Not the *least* you could do."

"I don't take your meaning," he said.

"Oh, I'm certain you do." She planted her hands upon the desk and leaned forward. "She's your answer, Drew. Don't let her slip away."

"I have every intention of paying a call upon

Miss Clarke once she's settled in London." The words felt stiff in his mouth.

"Don't be an idiot. She's not going to *settle* in London—she'll find employment and be gone. And I assure you, once that happens, your own sense of ducal standing will prevent you from doing what you should have done all along."

He narrowed his eyes. "I'll conduct my affairs without your interference, Viola, as ever. Thank you for your concern, and your consultation." He nodded at the hatbox. "Now, I must return to my work."

He flipped a page in the ledger and made a show of running his finger down the column, pretending to be intent on the numbers. With a snort of disapproval, Viola straightened and, when he still refused to look at her, stalked out of the study.

Once he was sure she'd gone, Drew let out a breath and leaned back in his chair.

Even if he made the leap, and asked Mena to consider him, would she agree? It was a precarious thing to do, especially given the enmity between their mothers. But their families were not the Montagues and Capulets, with blood and death standing in their way.

And surely there was no better season for forgiveness than Christmas.

Pushing back his chair, he stood. It was time

for a long-overdue conversation with the Duchess of Beckford.

"MOTHER?" Mena rapped on the door of Lady Marston's suite.

Her heart beat rapidly, and she had to quash the urge to retreat back to her own rooms and spare her mother the pain to come. But there had been too many secrets already, and this one would eat a hole in her soul if she continued to conceal it.

Lady Marston opened the door and gave her daughter a quizzical look. "Mena—is there something amiss?"

Mena swallowed back the dryness in her throat. "One might say so. May I come in?"

Her mother nodded and stepped back, and Mena went into the sitting room of the Ivory Suite. Her fingers, clenched about the incriminating papers, were cold.

"What more could possibly be going wrong?" Lady Marston asked with a frown. "Haven't we had enough trouble, of late?"

"Yes, and I'm sorry. Do sit down, Mother." Mena nodded to the settee drawn up on one side of the hearth.

Lady Marston settled on the cream-colored

upholstery, then patted the spot next to her. "Come. What are those?" She looked at the papers Mena was carrying. "Bad news from the solicitors? There is no money for us, after all?"

"Not quite that dire, but…"

Mena settled beside her mother and handed her the apology letter from the duchess. Best to begin with that, and then move on to the more difficult missive from Lord Marston.

Brows drawn together, Lady Marston began to read. Mena watched her mother's face closely, seeing the emotions flicker across her expression: impatience, surprise, and then dawning comprehension as she finished reading.

"Where did you find this?" Lady Marston demanded, flipping the letter over, then back again to study the date. "And when?"

"It was in the study at Marston Mews—and I just discovered it today, during our visit." She felt it best not to go into the details of how she'd broken into the room and rifled through the baron's desk. "Yesterday, I had a conversation with Lady Viola, who insisted her mother had, indeed, sent a letter of apology, which made me think… Well, at any rate, I found it. Along with this."

Mena extended Lord Marston's notes, the papers rustling slightly as her fingers trembled.

Oh, she desperately didn't want to show her mother how her own husband had conspired to break her friendship with the duchess. But it must be done.

As she read, Lady Marston's lips parted in surprise, and her face grew pale. She perused the pages once, twice, three times, before finally looking up at Mena.

"I'm sorry," was all Mena could manage.

"I never…" Her mother looked down at the ragged notes. "I never guessed that he would keep Lady Beckford's apology from me."

"Are you angry?"

Lady Marston met Mena's gaze. Her color was returning, along with a steely glint in her eyes.

"I must confess I am," she said. "A trifle, at least. And saddened to discover I'd thought wrongly of Lady Beckford for all these years."

"Perhaps not too wrongly," Mena said, thinking of the duchess's high-handed ways. "She might have tried writing you again, after all."

"A second letter wouldn't have reached me, either. I do believe your father was right to think Lord Beckford was opposed to my friendship with his wife. There were a number of instances where the duke made his opinion of my common origins quite clear." Lady

Marston shook her head. "The connection between our families has been unfortunate, all the way around."

"Not entirely," Mena said. "I have happy memories of Dovington." Not to mention current ones.

"Your happy times wouldn't have continued. Surely the present situation bears that out."

Mena stared at her mother. "What present situation?"

"Oh, Mena. Do you think I haven't noticed your fondness for Andrew Harrington? That's a path that will lead precisely nowhere."

"I'm not *fond* of him," Mena protested, but the heat rising to her cheeks surely betrayed her true feelings.

Her mother reached over and set a hand on Mena's arm. "As I said, nothing will come of it. The Harringtons are altogether too preoccupied with social status. And while I know you might suffer a bit, we'll be gone from here soon enough."

Mena jumped up and began pacing before the fire. How had the conversation suddenly come to be about her and Lord Beckford?

"Are you going to speak to the duchess?" she asked, trying to turn the tables. "Tell her you never received her apology?"

Lady Marston glanced down at the papers

in her lap. "Perhaps it's better if I don't. Let bygones be bygones."

"That's just cowardice."

"As is refusing to admit your feelings toward the duke," her mother said. "And both ultimately have the same outcome. Namely, no matter what we do or say, nothing will change. Why inflict further pain upon ourselves?"

"What if, once you and Lady Beckford reconciled, it would clear the way for..." Mena pulled in a breath, then continued her foolhardy thought. "For the duke to say something?"

"To offer for you, you mean?" Her mother's brows rose. "I'm sorry to put it so bluntly, my dear, but he wouldn't, even if matters were repaired between our families. He hasn't the vision, nor the courage—though if by some outside chance he did, I would certainly applaud him for it. After what transpired with the reprehensible Mr. Whittaker, you deserve a gentleman willing to bare his heart, no matter the disparities between you."

"It didn't do you and Father much good, in the end," Mena said, regretting the words as soon as they left her mouth.

Her mother looked at her sadly. "But it did. Lord Marston only wanted what was best for us. And though I cannot agree with some of his actions, I wouldn't have ever chosen otherwise. We were happy. I'll always be glad I married him. And I have a lovely daughter to care for now, even though he is gone."

She held her arms out to Mena.

Unable to hold back a sob, Mena threw herself onto the settee and into her mother's embrace.

"I'll take care of you now, Mother," she said, sniffling. "I promise. No matter what happens."

Her heart burned fiercely with the promise. Whatever the world held for them, they would face it as a family, and thrive. She must believe that to be true, even as the grim prospect of the New Year hovered in the wings, waiting to sweep them up into the ashes of a cold, gray future.

CHAPTER 12

On Christmas Eve day, Mena rose and, after a quick breakfast in her suite, headed to the kitchen at Dovington Hall.

The afternoon before, she'd met with the dour Mrs. Simpson, who had grudgingly introduced her to the chef: the voluble Monsieur Allard, who'd come with the family from London in order to preside over the holiday meals at Dovington Hall. And despite the housekeeper's disapproval, the chef had been delighted to allow Mena space in the kitchen to make her parkin.

He loaned her a voluminous apron, pausing now and then from his own preparations to watch with bright eyes as Mena mixed first the dry ingredients, then the wet, and then combined them. Despite the whirl of activity in the kitchen, he took a moment to taste a spoonful of the batter, and proclaimed it delicious.

"The treacle combined with the spices make a fine balance, *non*?" He brought his thumb and fingers together in an airy gesture of approval. "And using the meal of oats instead of wheat, this is traditional?"

"It's what makes Yorkshire parkin special." She slid the pan into one of the oven compartments of the huge cast-iron stove that dominated the back wall. "I'll return in half an hour to check on the baking."

"The cake will be ready to eat later in the day?" the chef asked.

"Yes—although it's even better after it sits for two or three days."

"In this household, I am afraid such sweets disappear too quickly." He gave her a conspiratorial smile. "The duke is fond of his cake."

"I know. I ought to have made a double batch."

"Next time, *cherie*."

There wouldn't be a next time, but Mena nodded anyway, folded up her apron, and thanked Monsieur Allard for allowing her use of his kitchen.

"It is no trouble. We are a gingerbread factory." He gestured to the side counter, where one of his underlings was hard at work piping royal icing onto dozens of gingerbread men. "For the tree. Mademoiselle Viola has grand dreams."

"Which she generally turns to reality," Mena observed.

"Indeed, she is a force of nature." The chef gave a small, admiring shake of his head.

The army of gingerbread men wasn't the only heroic undertaking, of course. One of the parlors had been entirely given over to three maids who'd been hard at work constructing silver-foil chains to drape about the tree. Viola had also sent to London for gilded almonds in dozens of ribbon-tied bags, an assortment of small toys to hang about the tree, and specially made tin candleholders to clip upon the branches, along with candles to fit them.

The entirety of Dovington Hall was redolent with festivity, and despite Mena's lingering melancholy, she couldn't help but be swept along. Viola had declared an exchange of gifts that evening, after the grand unveiling of the Christmas tree.

Mena's gift to the duke—*the whole household,* she reminded herself—would be the parkin cake. But she still wanted to give Viola something more. The duke's sister had made her an early present of an ivory chiffon sash delicately embroidered with flowers, which, as Viola had guessed, made a lovely complement to the gown Mena planned to wear that evening.

It was pleasant to have a frippery, although she hadn't been able to dissuade her mother from wearing her usual black. Lady Marston would mourn her husband in full, though she'd encouraged Mena to move to half mourning after six months.

"You're young," she'd said, "and it will better serve you to wear a bit of color when you make your inquiries."

Meaning that no one wanted to hire a governess or companion who sported nothing but the unrelieved black of full mourning.

As Mena stepped into the entrance hall, the sight of the Christmas tree shook her out of her sorry thoughts. Servants buzzed about it, draping the silver-paper chains in swoops between the evergreen branches. A footman perched on a ladder, hanging gingerbread men in the upper branches, while one of the maids leaned over the banister, alternately directing him to reach higher and exclaiming with worry for his safety.

"Begging your pardon, but you're not supposed to look yet, miss," another maid said to Mena, dropping her a nervous curtsey. "I'm sorry, but Lady Viola gave us strict instructions."

"I'll take the other stairs," Mena said, smiling. "One wouldn't want to run afoul of the duke's sister, after all."

"Oh, thank you," the maid said fervently, then whirled back to her chain-draping.

Halfway down the hall, Mena met the duke as he stepped out of his study.

"Good day, Miss Clarke," he said. "Where are you hurrying off to?"

"I'm headed back to my rooms," she said. "The front stairs are forbidden, just so you know."

"Are they?" His brows quirked up in amusement. "Well then, allow me to escort you up the back staircase. Unless that's closed off, too, and we must take the servants' way?"

"No. It's my understanding that your sister doesn't want any of us to see the tree until after dinner."

"Always full of secrets and surprises," he said, something flashing across his face that made Mena think he had a secret or surprise of his own.

"What are you up to?" she asked, narrowing her eyes at him.

"Not a thing." He held out his arm to her, then leaned closer, studying her face. "You've a bit of flour on your cheek. Speaking of surprises."

"You weren't supposed to know," she said crossly, wiping at her face.

He pursed his lips in pretend innocence. "Know what? You've missed it, by the way. Closer to your chin."

She swiped again, and he shook his head.

"Let me." He reached his hand out, cupped her cheek, and gently brushed his thumb across the corner of her lips.

Mena froze, sensation flaring through her like a wick catching fire. He'd touched her face, but her entire body was filled with sparks.

Their gazes met, held, and she heard his breathing hitch, as though he'd been running. His fingers were warm on her skin, his hazel eyes filled with gold flecks.

Then a footman turned the corner, and Drew pulled his hand away.

"I agree, Miss Clarke, that the tree will be something to behold. Shall we?"

"Certainly." With a bright, false smile pasted on her face, Mena set her hand on his arm.

They passed the footman, who stepped aside and bowed as they went down the hallway. Surely he hadn't witnessed that moment when—Well, Mena hardly knew how to describe it. All the duke had done was brush flour from her face, yet it felt as though her heart had nearly stopped beating.

For his part, Drew hadn't seemed entirely unaffected either.

They mounted the stairs without speaking, and Mena tried not to think too much about his touch, or his laughter, or the fact that in a mere two days he'd be going back to London and the enchanted holiday bubble she'd been dwelling in must burst.

"I hope your mother is recovered," he said as they approached the door to Mena's suite. "Will she be joining us for dinner?"

For the past few days, everyone had pretended to the polite fiction that Lady Marston felt unwell in the evenings and found it necessary to take a tray in her rooms. Interestingly enough, the duchess seemed to suffer from the opposite malady and was unable to join them for luncheon. And breakfast was left entirely to the younger set.

But Mena, for her part, was thoroughly tired of pretense.

"She will," she said firmly. "It's Christmas Eve, after all."

"I hope both of you will also join us for carols in the music room this afternoon. The duchess will provide accompaniment on the pianoforte. And if we're lucky, Viola won't touch her harp."

Mena shot him a look. "Surely she's not

dreadful. How can anyone sound bad upon the harp?"

"And yet she manages." Drew shook his head in mock sadness. "Until then, Miss Clarke."

"Your Grace." She dipped him a curtsey, then slipped into her rooms before she did something entirely foolish, like confess her feelings. Or go up on her toes and kiss him.

No, she told herself sternly, standing with her back against the closed door.

Drew might be her childhood friend, but far beyond that, he was the Duke of Beckford. She must remember it—and the gulf between their stations—at all costs. Doing otherwise would only scar her already battered heart beyond repair.

Unfortunately, she feared it was already too late.

THE PARKIN TURNED OUT PERFECTLY—RICH brown and fragrant with ginger and mace. Once the cake cooled, Mena cut it into squares and tucked portions into the assorted small tins one of the scullery maids had found for her. There was just enough to go around, with one piece left over, which she presented to Monsieur Allard in thanks.

"I shall endeavor to save it for the recommended three days," he said, lifting the parkin to his nose and inhaling appreciatively. "But I fear it will be difficult."

He gave Mena a basket to transport the tins of parkin back up to her room, where she tied a scarlet ribbon about each one. She also chose a book from her small collection to give to Viola —the Christmas tale *The Cricket on the Hearth* by Dickens. It was a sweet story, and she hoped the duke's sister wasn't already in possession of the volume.

If she was, Mena supposed Viola could always leave the extra copy at Dovington.

Her Christmas surprises finished, Mena curled up in one of the chairs beside the fire, savoring the moment of solitude. It had been a fraught several days, and she wanted nothing more than to watch the flames dance in the hearth and sip the cup of tea she'd had the maid deliver.

And not think about the future, or the past, or anything but the snow now falling softly around Dovington Hall, cocooning them in quiet white.

CHAPTER 13

"Your chef has outdone himself," Theo said to Drew as the servants brought out the main course of the Christmas Eve dinner.

Their meal had begun with leek soup, then pheasant pie, and now the footmen were carrying round a poached salmon and delivering individually baked servings of Yorkshire pudding.

"Wait until tomorrow," Drew said to his brother. "Goose with all the trimmings."

Theo laughed. "You'll have to roll me back to London. Good thing my cook isn't as talented as Monsieur Allard. I don't suppose I might bribe him away?"

"Never," Drew said with a smile.

He was in a fine mood, despite the very real possibility that his hopes would come crashing down later that night. The table sparkled with crystal and silver, the gold-chased china gleamed, and the conversation had been lively and convivial. His mother and Lady Marston had even acknowledged one another's presences, Drew was pleased to note.

The duchess was seated on his right, across from Theo, with Viola next to her, Lady Marston across, and Mena beside her mother.

Mena. Miss Philomena Clarke. He couldn't help glancing at her frequently. Each time their gazes met, his hopes spiked. Along with his worry, of course—but there was no point in dwelling on possible sorrow when there was so much joy in front of him.

Earlier, during the carol singing, he'd contrived to stand next to her. She had a pretty alto voice, as did Lady Marston, and the combined families had, in his opinion, sounded quite musical together.

Until Viola had seated herself at the harp, which was not quite in tune with the piano. That, and her less-than-impeccable timing with the chords, had been enough to dissolve both himself and Theo into laughter.

"The Merry Gentlemen will get no rest, at this rate," Theo had said. "Please, Viola, stop plunking. I beg you."

"She has improved from last year," Lady Beckford said, looking up from the keyboard.

"It's not *that* dreadful," Mena had added, sending Drew an apologetic look.

"I've delivered to you an astoundingly beautiful tree," Viola said, unaffected by her brothers' teasing. "Therefore, you must indulge me. Shall we sing 'Joy to the World'?"

They managed, despite Viola's chaotic playing. Drew noted, however, that Mena's eyes grew wider with every verse.

"Don't worry," he said quietly, leaning close to her ear when they finished. "It's always this bad—if not worse."

"Oh," she said, blinking.

"Final song," Theo declared. "A nice, loud rendition of 'I Saw Three Ships Come Sailing In.' Ready?"

He raised his hands and led them through an ever-speeding performance of the carol that ended with nearly everyone laughing instead of singing. Lady Marston was smiling, and even the duchess's lips had softened in amusement.

"You see," Viola had said, rising from her harp. "That was marvelous."

The general humor had continued through the early evening with a quick bout of charades, and then dinner. And now that the servants were taking up their plates, it was time for Viola's grand spectacle.

"No removing for port, gentlemen," she said, giving Drew and Theo a pointed look. "Unless you want it served to everyone as we view the tree."

"There's a thought," Theo said, glancing at the duchess. "Mother?"

"I suppose," she said. "It is Christmas Eve, after all."

"It is, indeed." Viola set her napkin aside and stood, and the rest of the table followed. "And now, I shall escort you all to the front of the house, where I'm sure any number of surprises are waiting to be unveiled."

She raised her brows at Drew, then turned with a swish of red satin skirts and led the way from the dining room. Theo followed, the duchess on his arm.

"Ladies," Drew said, extending his right arm to Lady Marston and his left to Mena. "Allow me to escort you both."

"How gentlemanly," Lady Marston said with an approving nod.

"I'm not certain we'll all three fit through the doorway." Despite the doubtful tone of her voice, Mena placed her hand on his sleeve.

"I'll go first," her mother said, and suited action to words, whisking ahead of them.

On their way out of the dining room, Drew directed the head footman to bring the tawny port and six glasses to the entrance hall. Then, folding his hand over Mena's, he led her at a sedate pace down the corridor. Her mother seemed content to continue on ahead of them. It was, he hoped, a harbinger of things to come.

"No racing?" Mena shot him a mischievous look.

She looked quite fetching in her lavender gown trimmed with ivory lace, a matching sash at her waist, and her hair caught up in an elegant coiffure.

"While I would certainly win," he said, forcing himself to stop staring at her and glancing ahead of them down the hall, "there are a few obstacles in the way. I wouldn't mind barreling over Theo and Viola, but our mothers are another matter."

"They certainly are." Mena let out a small sigh, then gave a shake of her head. "And *I* would have won—but don't worry, I believe there's a consolation prize waiting for you."

"I certainly hope so." Though he was holding out for a far greater prize than a piece of cake.

At the end of the corridor, the servants had rigged up a curtain across the opening to the entrance hall. Viola paused and poked her head around the edge of the heavy fabric. When she reemerged, she was smiling broadly.

"Ladies and gentlemen," she said grandly. "I present to you…the Christmas tree!"

A servant pulled the curtain aside to reveal the result of all the servants' hard work. Drew had to admit that it was an amazing spectacle. The enormous evergreen rose to the ceiling, shining with candles as though a hundred tiny stars had come to rest upon the branches. The silver-foil chains glittered, and the toys and sweets hanging from the branches had a magical sheen, as though they were mystical treasures brought from afar.

Beside him, Mena let out an awed breath.

On Viola's orders, the maids had earlier gathered up all the presents to be exchanged, which were now placed artfully around the base of the tree. Drew spotted the hatbox, several beribboned tins, and a number of smaller items wrapped in brown paper, some decorated with ribbons, some with silver-foil cutouts of snowflakes.

"Come, come," Viola said, gesturing the party to the six chairs placed in a semicircle facing the tree. "It's time for the presents. Mother, you are here in the middle, along with Lady Marston. Theo, there, Drew and Mena on the other side. I'll be acting as your courier and delivering the gifts."

"You've missed your calling as a shepherdess," Theo said wryly, but he took his place without protest.

The older ladies paused and looked at one another, neither of them moving toward their indicated seats. Drew leaned forward, and Mena's grip on his arm tightened.

It was a brave move on Viola's part to seat their mothers together—but then, the evening called for boldness. And after his conversation with the duchess, Drew hoped for the best, on all counts. Still, it was a tense moment.

"I would be…delighted," Lady Marston finally said, her tone cautious.

"As would I," the duchess said, more firmly. She took a half step back and extended her hand toward Mena's mother. "After you?"

"Thank you." Lady Marston took her seat, and the duchess settled beside her.

Drew exhaled softly. That was one hurdle jumped. He exchanged a quick, relieved look with Mena, then escorted her to her assigned chair.

❄

Mena settled on the velvet-upholstered seat, her heart beating as if she truly *had* raced down the corridor. She didn't know if she was nervous about the fact of her mother and the duchess actually speaking to one another, or if the majestic tree had dazzled her senses, or if she should attribute her unsteadiness of emotion to the gentleman seated on her left.

All evening, Drew had been giving her looks, and she scarcely knew what to think. Had Viola told him about the letters? She'd sworn not to, and Mena believed she was a woman of her word—but there was no question there were secrets simmering in the duke's hazel eyes.

It didn't help matters that he looked ridiculously handsome in his dark coat and trousers, a bronze brocade waistcoat, and a topaz stickpin winking from the folds of his impeccably tied cravat.

"Now," Viola said, standing before their small assembly and clasping her hands together, "how shall we begin?"

"I have a gift I would like to bestow," the duchess said, gesturing. "It is the small box there, on the left."

Viola retrieved the box, which was fashioned of rosewood with gold clasp and hinges. A jewelry box of some sort, Mena guessed, perhaps containing a present for the duchess's daughter.

"Where shall I deliver it?" Viola asked with a mischievous smile.

"You may hand it to me." Lady Beckford held out an imperious hand.

When it was in her grasp, the duchess turned to Mena's mother, who had gone very still.

"This gift..." Lady Beckford drew in a breath, then continued. "This gift has been ten years in the giving. I hope you will accept it in the spirit of renewed friendship."

She lifted the lid of the box to reveal a pair of silver-framed cameos nestled against a black velvet lining. The brooches were each a woman's face in profile, delicately carved of shell and mounted upon a dark blue background. They were placed facing away from one another, but the duchess lifted them out, reversing the direction as she held them in her palms.

"I had these made after our falling-out," she said to Lady Marston. "They have sat in darkness, refusing to look at one, another for far too long. Will you accept my apology?"

She held out her hand, offering Mena's mother one of the brooches.

Mena bit her lip. *Take it,* she silently urged.

Lady Marston blinked twice, in rapid succession, and Mena saw the telltale brightness of tears in her mother's eyes. Yet she hesitated.

"I am sorry," the duchess said, her fingers slowly closing over the brooch. "I was wrong—I knew it all along, but my own stubborn pride..." She cleared her throat delicately. "I don't blame you for never responding to my overtures. After such a grievous wronging, you had every right to cut off our friendship."

"I never received your letter," Lady Marston said, her back as straight as a poker. "That is, not until yesterday. If I had, things might have been different. But tell me, what made you change your mind?"

The duchess glanced at Drew, the merest ghost of a smile crossing her lips. "I had an illuminating, if somewhat difficult, conversation with my son."

Mena's mother tilted her head to one side. Then, ever so slowly, she reached out and lifted the cameo from Lady Beckford's outstretched hand.

"Very well," she said. "I accept your apology."

Mena sagged with relief. Beside her, Drew let out a gusty breath, while Theo grinned and Viola squeaked in glee.

"Thank goodness!" Viola put her hand to

her heart. "I was about to perish from the suspense."

Mena nodded at her, sharing the same reaction, though not quite so dramatically expressed.

"That's enough theatrics," the duchess said, giving her daughter a look of mild reproof, then turning back to Lady Marston. "Thank you."

They clasped forearms in a brief embrace, and Mena swallowed back the lump of emotion in her throat. Their reconciliation was proof that, sometimes, things could turn out happily, after all.

"Port," the duke said, beckoning to the footman who stood near the wall holding a tray filled with glasses of the amber liquid.

"Absolutely." Theo took a glass and, as soon as everyone had one in hand, hoisted it in the air. "A toast! To friendship."

"Indeed." Drew held his glass out to Mena and, smiling, she clinked it with hers.

She couldn't stop smiling, in fact, especially when her mother and the duchess took turns pinning on their new brooches.

"My present next," the duke said, gesturing to his sister. "Deliver the hatbox, if you please."

Viola picked up the box and brought it to Mena, handing it over with a sly grin. Mena glanced at Drew. Surely this couldn't be a re-placement for her ruined hat? If so, then he'd gone to a great deal of trouble and expense on her account. Her heart gave a little flutter at the thought.

"Open it," he said softly.

She untied the ribbons and lifted the lid, then gazed down in amazement at the up-turned velvet brim, the profusion of silk roses.

"It's almost exactly the same. However did you do it?"

"I have my ways," he said.

"Ahem." Viola tapped her foot meaningfully upon the marble floor.

"And my sister's gracious help," Drew added.

Mena lifted the hat and held it up, admiring the pristine velvet, the uncrumpled roses.

"They're not precisely the same color, are they?" he asked, a touch ruefully.

"They're better," she said, and meant it. "Thank you—I will treasure this."

Her old hat was a memory of a former time, a former self. And while that one had been ru-ined by the elements, Mena felt that, on bal-ance, she herself had emerged stronger for the adversity. However uncomfortable her future, she had renewed hope—a slightly different shade, perhaps, but flowering all the same.

"Who's next?" Viola asked.

"If you would fetch the tins," Mena said. "I've a little something for each of you."

"Finally." Drew rubbed his hands together. "I've been waiting for this."

"Lemon tarts?" she asked with mock innocence.

"Of course—my favorite." He winked at her as his sister handed the tins around, keeping the last one for herself.

Drew had the bow untied and the lid off in a trice. Lifting a square of parkin, he nodded sagely. "An excellent heft to it, and the fragrance is most enticing."

"Oh, just take a bite," Viola said.

He obeyed, closing his eyes momentarily as he chewed. Everyone else watched him, which Mena thought would have been amusing, if not for her unaccountable nervousness.

"Well?" Theo asked, one eyebrow raised.

Drew opened his eyes and shook his head. "Dreadful. I think it's best if you give all your tins to me, so that I might spare you the terrible experience. No, no—no need to open them and sample. You may take my word for it."

"Quite delicious, then," Theo said. "I expected as much."

"You are a rascal," the duchess said. "Really, Drew, can't you be serious?"

"I can." He set his tin of parkin down. "But first, I would like to tell you all a story."

"There are still presents," Viola said, glancing at the tree.

"Not to mention a trove of sweets and toys," Theo said. "Whatever are we to do with all of that?"

"I had a thought." Drew's gaze skimmed his siblings and settled on his mother. "What if we were to invite Baron Marston and his brood over, tomorrow afternoon? The children would certainly appreciate the Christmas tree."

The duchess pursed her lips. "That's rather" —she stopped, looked the bountifully laden tree up and down, then turned back to her son —"kind of you. If Viola agrees to the plundering, then I shall lend my approval."

"It's a grand idea." Viola clapped her hands. "Indeed, I had that very thought myself. Now, what is this story you mean to tell us, Drew?"

"Gather round," he said, rather unnecessarily, as they were already in a close semicircle. "I have a tale to relate of a prince who lived in a faraway kingdom."

"I hope this tale isn't overlong," Theo said, then subsided at his mother's stern look.

"Once upon a time," Drew began, "there lived a prince—"

"So you've said," Viola interrupted.

"—who was required to choose a bride. All the ladies of the court were well aware that the time had come for the duke—er, the *prince*—to make a match. They simpered and cooed like a flock of useless, pretty birds, hoping to catch his eye and become the next princess. The prince was nearly in despair, until a clever thought came to him. 'Very well,' he declared, 'I will wed whichever girl can bake the most delicious cake with her own two hands.' He would sample the cakes one night hence, and make his choice."

"I think I know where this story is leading," Theo murmured.

Mena's mother set a hand on her shoulder. For her part, Mena's chest felt tight, as though her corset laces had suddenly squeezed the breath from her lungs. Surely Drew wasn't… Surely he wasn't implying…

"This announcement caused a great deal of consternation among the ladies, as you might imagine." He nodded at his listeners. "For you see, none of these noble ladies had ever set foot in a kitchen, let alone knew how to cook. All except one, the only daughter of a minor nobleman. You see, her grandmother had been a commoner, and had passed the secret family recipe of ginger cake down to her granddaughter, instructing her well in its baking."

Drew sent Mena a sidelong smile that made her shiver with disbelief. With hope.

Mena's mother's fingers tightened upon her shoulder. "Breathe," she whispered.

I'm trying, Mena wanted to reply, but her mouth seemed unable to form words.

"To keep the young ladies from cheating," Drew continued, "the prince dispatched his trusted servants to oversee their baking efforts and ensure none of them received aid from trained pastry chefs and the like. At the appointed hour, the ladies assembled at the palace to present their cakes to the prince."

"He sounds like a clever fellow," Theo said.

"He was," his brother replied. "Though he regretted his cleverness as he tasted the results of the ladies' baking efforts. The first cake was horribly sweet and yet sour at the same time. The second was full of unbaked lumps of flour. The third was as flat and hard as a brick, and so on, until the poor prince thought he might never eat another bite of sweets again, so unappetizing were the samples."

"Unfortunate," his mother said dryly. "But he did bring it upon himself."

Mena could only stare at Drew, heart racing, as he continued his tale.

"A scent reached the prince's nose, warm and tempting, with hints of ginger and treacle.

The last young woman stood before him, holding a plate of molasses-brown cake that matched the sweetness of her eyes. Her name was Miranda"—at this, Viola let out a snort, which Drew ignored—"and of all the ladies of the court, he recalled that she was the one who would race him down the hallways, stand shoulder to shoulder with him to defeat their winter enemies, and treat him not like a rarified prince, but as a person."

Drew turned to Mena and took her hands, which, despite her efforts at composure, were trembling. His fingers were reassuringly warm around hers, and she felt the hot sting of tears rise to her eyes.

"The prince," he said softly, "took a bite of the cake. It was perfect, and he closed his eyes, the better to savor it. Seeing this, the other ladies began to jeer at Miranda, thinking she had failed just like them. But the prince rose from the table and rounded it. Then, before the assembled nobles, he took her hands and went down on one knee."

Suiting action to words, Drew slipped out of his chair to kneel before Mena. Her mother gasped, and Viola brought her clasped hands up to her chin.

Mena was alight, like the tree rising before

them, full of a thousand little flames flickering and dancing.

"I have a question," Drew said, looking up at her expectantly.

"A question… Is this part of the story?" she managed to ask.

"It is—the prince's story, and my own. May I ask it?"

Gaze fixed on his, she nodded slowly. Part of her still couldn't believe this was happening —that the Duke of Beckford was down on his knee before her, about to ask for her hand.

It *was* a fairy tale, and somehow she'd slipped inside it. Or had too much port and fallen asleep under the tree, and at any moment would wake to discover it was all a dream.

But the feel of Drew's fingers clasping hers was real, the taut silence of the onlookers, the mingled scents of evergreen and gingerbread wafting from the tree.

"Miss Philomena Clarke," Drew said, holding her gaze. "Would you do me the very real honor of consenting to be my wife?"

Mena squeezed her eyes shut, feeling a tear slip down her cheek. Drew's grasp tightened. Her mother, still holding her shoulder, clutched hard, then let go.

With a deep breath—as deep as Mena could

manage, given that she was full of nothing but shimmering light—she opened her eyes.

"Yes," she said. "Yes, Drew Harrington, I will marry you."

"I'm so glad," he said softly. "I didn't want to lose you again."

Theo sprang to his feet with a whoop, and Viola let out an exclamation of relief.

"Thank heavens," she said. "I was worried there for a moment."

Mena glanced at her mother, relieved to see approval shining from Lady Marston's eyes. Even the duchess seemed glad, giving her a regal nod of consent.

Still on one knee, Drew released Mena's hands and reached into the pocket of his waist-coat. He pulled out a ring—a square-cut emerald surrounded by diamonds that caught the light like sparkles on new snow.

"My duchess," he said, slipping it on her finger.

She stared down at the brilliant gems, momentarily shocked. "Oh, yes—I suppose I'm to be a duchess now."

"That's generally the case when one agrees to marry a duke." Drew gave her a crooked smile. "I hope it doesn't bother you too greatly."

"As long as no one bars me from an occasional baking foray into the kitchen."

"They wouldn't dare—especially after tasting your parkin cake."

"You didn't propose to me just because of that, surely?" Mena asked, recalling his story.

"Not at all." His expression stilled, his hazel eyes solemn. "I proposed to you because I love you, Mena. But surely you knew that."

"I'd hoped." She leaned toward him until their foreheads nearly touched. "I must confess that I love you too. And have done so for a very long time, though I tried to forget it."

The smile was back in his eyes as he lifted her hand and dropped a kiss upon the back, just below the sparkling gems upon her finger.

"Isn't that the family ring?" Viola asked, glancing at her mother. "You knew?"

The duchess gave her a smug look. "As I said, your brother and I had a most edifying conversation, upon a variety of subjects."

"Congratulations, my dear." Mena's mother leaned over and kissed her cheek. "I am so happy for you."

Theo raised his port glass. "Another toast," he said. "To family."

"To new sisters!" Viola said.

"And old friends." The duchess clinked her glass with Lady Marston.

"Forgiveness," Mena's mother added with a nod.

"New beginnings," Mena said, locking gazes with Drew.

"Most importantly," he said, "to love."

"Love," they echoed, even as it flew about them all, warm and bright—the eternal message, passed down through the centuries.

Love.

IN THE MOOD for more sweet holiday romance? Don't miss **Noble Holidays**, a complete collection of heartwarming Christmas tales.

NEW YEAR'S FORTUNE

A VICTORIAN NEW YEAR'S STORY

London, December 31ˢᵗ, 1852

Mr. Philip Plumley finished applying boot blacking to his hair and then stared woefully at his reflection. Alas. Instead of transforming his appearance into that of a striking, dark-haired gentleman, his features—which he considered far too round of cheek and long of nose—seemed fundamentally unaltered.

Except that, instead of his usual mop of fair hair, a greasy black creature squatted atop his head.

"Blast," he said softly, scrubbing a runnel of blacking from his cheek.

Perhaps he oughtn't to appear at Miss Violet

Thornton's doorstep that evening, after all. But his heart gave a rather severe pang at the thought, and he just as quickly abandoned the notion of staying in. It was New Year's Eve, after all. Only the most dreary sops refused to venture out, when there was so much festivity to be had.

He glanced about his small bachelor flat. It was cold—but that was his own fault, for clearing out the hearth first thing that morning. But starting the year with the old ashes swept out was considered good luck. And currently, he was rather in need of as much luck as he could muster.

Thus the hair blacking, although that was more to benefit Miss Violet than himself.

Of course, it *would* reflect well on him if he were to bestow the blessing of the first footing. Tradition held that the first person over the threshold on the new year should, ideally, be a handsome, dark-haired fellow. Philip was doing his best to come up to scratch.

He only prayed that his rival, Thomas Millerton, would not be there, vying for Miss Violet's attention. Millerton's hair was black as a crow's wing, and Philip gritted his teeth at the fact.

Still, there was no helping it, except with a bit of artificial color. At least, while he was out and about, the mess on top of his head would be adequately concealed by his top hat.

The small clock atop his currently cold mantel dinged the hour, chiming out eleven tinny strokes. He'd best make haste, if he wanted to arrive at the Thornton's by midnight. Leaving his dispiriting reflection behind, he donned his overcoat and squished his hat atop his head.

Unfortunately, once he gained the street, he realized he'd made a mistake. There were no cabs at all to be found. Curse himself for an idiot! Of course—everyone in London was on their way to one event or another.

He consulted his pocket watch, grimly calculating the time and distance. If he walked at a brisk clip, he should be able to reach Manning Square with a few minutes to spare. He glanced at the low scruff of clouds over the city, praying the rain would hold off, Then, jamming his hands into his coat pockets, he set out.

Manning Square was still a few blocks away when the drizzle began. As usual, he'd forgotten his umbrella. With a grimace, Philip turned up his collar and lengthened his stride. The blister forming on his right heel pained him with every other step, and he was breathing a bit heavily with effort when he finally sighted his destination.

He paused on the street corner across from the Thornton's town house and, by the flickering light of the gas lamp overhead, opened his watch. Rain slicked the glass, and he wiped it impatiently away. Three minutes til midnight. He sagged with relief—he'd made it just in time.

As he stepped off the curb, a cab turned the corner, its wheels splashing up a plume of water.

"Watch out!" Philip yelled, leaping back.

He was not quick enough to keep his trousers dry. and immediately an unpleasant dampness seeped through the wool.

The cab slowed, and for a moment he wondered if the driver meant to apologize. But no, it was only stopping to let a passenger out.

Directly in front of the Thornton's house.

Apprehension slithered a bony hand around his heart. Then squeezed, as Thomas Millerton alighted, gave the driver a jaunty tip of his hat, and bounded up the stairs.

Philip finished crossing the street with a confused notion of tackling Millerton to the ground. He was still several paces away as his rival lifted the knocker.

Then, with a clamor of metal against metal, all the bells in London began to ring. Some near, with a sonorous tolling, others only a high distant echo. Even through the din, Philip could hear his own hopes cracking in two.

Windows and doors were thrown open, and cries of "Happy New Year" resounded through the square.

The Thornton's door swung wide and Thomas Millerton sauntered inside, secure in the knowledge that he'd brought a year's worth of good luck to the household.

Philip stared after him. He should leave. Surely there would be cabs aplenty for the next quarter hour. Unless all the cabbies and their horses had snuck away for a celebration of their own. A raindrop crawled coldly down the back of his neck, and he sighed.

Then Violet Thornton's laughter threaded gaily out into the street, and Philip straightened.

His rival might have beat him across the threshold, but Millerton did not have much to recommend himself, other than a too-handsome face and a glib way with words.

Philip, on the other hand, was a clerk at the Bank of England. He considered himself a steady, respectable fellow who would make a solid husband to some agreeable young woman.

Namely, Miss Violet Thornton.

Shaking the rain from his shoulders, he

took the last few steps to the Thornton's still-open front door.

"Happy New Year, sir," the butler greeted him. "Your hat?"

Philip tried to ignore the way the man stared at him as he doffed his top hat. He divested himself of his overcoat as well, and then, wet pants and all, limped his way into the drawing room.

A number of young ladies and gentlemen were seated about the room, engaged in conversation and drinking punch. Violet Thornton's mother was stationed at the door, a sharp-eyed chaperone.

"Why, Mr. Plumley," she said brightly. "Welcome. And what a… unique manner of dressing your hair."

The other guests glanced up, and several of them laughed, Miss Violet among them. Philip felt himself flush—but also noted he wasn't the only fair-haired fellow who had darkened his locks for the evening.

"Happy New Year," he said. "As you might guess, I was hoping for first footing."

"Too late, old chap," Millerton said, lifting his cup of punch. "Maybe next year. My, but you look a sight."

More laughter. At the side of the room, Philip noticed someone urgently beckoning to him. He glanced over to see Miss Daisy Thornton, Violet's younger sister. She met his gaze and widened her eyes, then jerked her head in the direction of the hall.

She was a flighty little thing, and he'd never paid her much mind. But the entreaty in her eyes roused his curiosity.

"Please excuse me for a moment," he said.

"Of course." Mrs. Thornton gave him an overbroad smile.

Philip retreated to the hallway, and in a moment Miss Daisy was there.

"Mr. Plumley, have you seen yourself?" she asked, doing away with any pleasantries.

"Not recently," he replied. "What is the matter?"

"I can't be gone for long, but come." She whirled and marched down the hall to the washroom.

Philip followed, now more than a little afraid of encountering his own reflection. When they reached the washroom, Miss Daisy stepped aside and gestured for him to enter.

"I'll bring hot water, and laundry soap," she said. "And extra towels. I'll knock thrice. Good luck."

Gingerly, Philip stepped inside and closed the door behind him. Then, holding his breath, he approached the looking glass mounted over the low basin.

Damnation.

The rain, and his exertions, had made the boot blacking run. He looked like nothing more than a chimney sweep, his forehead and cheeks smeared with ashes, the sides of his neck the color of coal.

Soap, Miss Daisy had said, and towels. Yes. He'd have to do his best to clean up the mess he'd made of himself. No wonder they'd been laughing at him.

He stripped off his coat, waistcoat, and shirt, noting the black stains around the collar, then bent over the basin. The ewer on the nearby stand held cool water, and he shivered as he bent and poured it over his head. A stream of inky water swirled down the drain.

A small soap, shaped like a rose, lay in a porcelain dish, but he didn't dare touch it with his blackened hands. He poured until the ewer was empty, then felt about for the small towel he'd seen hung beneath the sink.

Three sharp raps came at the door.

"A moment," Philip called, straightening and swiping the towel across his face.

"Hurry," Miss Daisy said from the hallway. "I can't stand here all night, you know."

He pulled the door open, and she thrust a pile of towels into his hands.

"There's a bar of lye soap on top," she said. "Try to keep it out of your eyes. And trade pitchers with me."

He set the towels aside, then grabbed the empty ewer and handed it to her, accepting one brimming with warm water in return.

"Thank you," he said. "I am greatly in your debt."

"You're most welcome." She blushed fiercely and would not meet his eyes, and after a belated moment he realized he was still shirtless.

Stammering an apology, he quickly shut the door. Why, oh why, had it not been Miss Violet who glimpsed him half-naked? It seemed his luck would never turn.

A quarter hour later, smelling strongly of lye, he rejoined the party in the drawing room. His hair was still a peculiar ashy shade, but at least he was no longer dripping boot blacking.

Mrs. Thornton raised her eyebrows approvingly and directed him to the refreshment table. He obediently fetched a glass of punch and a biscuit, then managed to find a seat near Miss Violet.

To his dismay, Thomas Millerton was seated at her side, and kept giving her bold looks that Philip could not approve of.

The room emptied out, as the various visitors departed for their own homes, and at last Philip realized that he ought to take his leave. It would be all too easy to stay there until dawn, gazing upon Miss Violet—even with that blighter Millerton there—but he'd be back again on the morrow.

New Year's Day was for paying calls. Though this time, he did not intend to walk all the way to Manning Square. Not that his poor abused heel would survive the journey.

"Good evening to you all," he said, rising. "Or, perhaps I ought to say, good morning."

Miss Violet blinked at him, but Miss Daisy let out a short laugh. At least someone found him amusing. A pity it wasn't the object of his affections.

He took Miss Violet's languidly offered hand and bowed over it. Then, for good measure, he did the same for Miss Daisy.

Strangely, their eyes met, and held, and an odd sensation burned in his belly. Perhaps he'd had an overabundance of punch.

The rain had stopped, he was glad to see when he stepped outside. A few stars shone through the gaps in the clouds, and it was a simple matter to hail one of the numerous cabs now roaming the neighborhoods.

As he entered the cold confines of his flat,

the clock on the mantel let out two dings. He was too weary to rekindle the fire. Tomorrow would be soon enough. Or, he thought with a rueful laugh, today.

THE NEW YEAR dawned clear and cold. Upon waking, Philip was obliged to push a pile of coats and trousers off his bed before he could rise. Sometime in the wee hours he'd woken overly chilled, and heaped his extra clothing atop the covers.

It had done the job, although he feared his wardrobe was a bit wrinkled. Shivering, he searched for a presentable set of garments, then, adequately dressed, went to build a fire. As the first touch of warmth seeped into the air, Philip opened the door of his flat and retrieved the breakfast the landlady set out.

It was the usual. A pot of tea, swaddled in a dishtowel to keep it warm—which, sadly, was less than effective—and a basket containing three hard scones, a wedge of cheddar, and an apple that was only slightly withered.

He brought the bounty inside and set it on the small table, then fetched his teacup painted with yellow roses and the matching plate from the shelf beside the washbasin. He lived very simply; some might say even parsimoniously, but he didn't mind.

His needs were scant, and he'd managed to save a great deal of his modest salary over the past few years. Enough to make a comfortable start, once he wed.

Not to mention his recent, unexpected inheritance from a distant uncle—though that had turned out to be rather underwhelming. Still, unlooked-for assets were never unwelcome, even if they consisted of a ramshackle cottage in Shropshire and a mere twenty pounds.

The tea, though lukewarm, was pleasantly strong. As he drank it and ate his scones, he pondered how best to ask for Miss Violet Thornton's hand.

He'd been calling upon her for the past eight months, ever since the Spring Cotillion where they'd first met. One of the other bank clerks, himself newly married, was of the opinion that everyone should enter that blissful state of matrimony. Thus, Philip had been introduced to Mrs. Thornton and her two daughters.

Violet was the elder, and so beautiful she made him dizzy. Black-haired and blue-eyed, her face was sweetly rounded with a pert nose and lips that he—most ungentlemanly—imagined kissing on a regular basis.

She'd allowed him to dance with her, and agreed, with her mother's permission, that he might call upon her. Thus had begun his regular pilgrimages to Manning Square.

It had been his intention to claim the first footing, then return on New Year's Day and, after securing her father's permission, ask Violet if she would make him the luckiest man in England by consenting to marry him. That, he'd thought, would be a clever twist on the theme of luck.

But that knave Millerton had stolen the advantage right out from under his nose.

Philip finished his tea and squinted at the dregs. He wished he could read whatever fortune the leaves imparted.

Perhaps he ought to make Miss Violet a gift of tea. A tin of Earl Grey would be refined, yet understated. Too understated?

Come to think of it, didn't Miss Violet take milk in her tea? He couldn't quite recall, though he knew that Miss Daisy did not, for she'd brandished her lemon slice at him once while he was taking tea with them.

So, Earl Grey wouldn't do. No one wanted curdled milk in their tea, after all. Such a gift would send entirely the wrong message.

"Pomanders!" The cry of a vendor drifted

up to his window from the street below. "Sweeeet oranges, for your sweetheart!"

Usually he paid the sellers' calls no heed, but this one was entirely providential. A pomander would be just the thing.

Hastily, he ran a comb through his still-ashen hair and made a reasonable job of tying his neck-cloth. His coat had absorbed the boot blacking well enough, which was more than could be said for his best top hat. With a grimace, he set it aside and donned the shorter one, which, in his opinion, made him appear too small of stature.

He set his dishes outside the door for the landlady to clean, locked his door, then dashed down the stairs. Luckily, the pomander seller hadn't progressed too far down the street, and Philip was able to catch her—though he wished he'd put a plaster on his heel, for the back of his shoe still rubbed most uncomfortably.

"How much?" he asked, gesturing to her basket of pomanders.

"One and six." She lifted it higher for his perusal.

The basket was half-filled with oranges pleasingly decorated with a pattern of cloves stuck into the rinds. Each fruit bore a colorful bow on top, though he was sorry to see there were no purple ones.

"One and six? That's rather dear," he said.

"Dear for your dearie," the vendor said with a guffaw.

He stared at the oranges, wondering which color to choose. Finally he settled on red. It made a cheery complement to the bright peel.

"Well done, sir," the vendor said, pocketing the coins he handed her. "A Happy New Year to you."

"And to yourself." He tipped his hat, then, accompanied by the aroma of spice and citrus, went to hail a cab.

Manning Square was filled with gentlemen paying calls at various houses. Unlike the usual back-and-forthing the ladies performed with one another—morning visiting hours, luncheons, afternoon teas—New Year's was the province of the men.

A number of them bore bouquets, and Philip castigated himself for not thinking of it. He was going to visit a young lady named after a flower, and he had not thought to bring her a posy of her namesake blossoms?

Though, truthfully, he found the smell of violets not to his taste. Luckily, the nose numbed to them quickly.

The butler admitted him to the Thornton's town house, this time without any untoward looks at his hair, beyond a quick waggle of the brows. Really, the man ought to learn how to school his expression.

As Philip stepped into the drawing room, he was momentarily assaulted by the scent of violets. Miss Violet herself sat before at least a half-dozen of the purple-hued bouquets.

It seemed his idea was not, perhaps, as original as he'd thought. Gratefully, he felt the nubbled texture of the pomander bulging in his coat pocket. He would present it to her with a flourishing bow, he decided. And perhaps a few words about her sweet nature, which graced everyone in the vicinity, like the aroma of—

Miss Violet brought a purple-ribboned cloved orange up to her nose and made a show of sniffing it.

"I am surrounded by the most delicious scents," she said, smiling at the man seated across from her. "Thank you, Mr. Millerton, for your most thoughtful gift. I must admit, I prefer it to the endless bouquets."

Philip's hand closed tightly around the pomander in his pocket, the cloves no doubt making little dents in his palm.

"Hello, Mr. Plumley," Miss Daisy said, noting his arrival. "Happy New Year."

"To yourself, as well," he said, making her a bow.

She was alone on the settee with a single,

slightly wilted bunch of daisies on the table before her. No profusion of bright flowers for the youngest sister; but despite that fact, she gave him a cheery smile.

Moved by the memory of her kindness to him the night before, he retrieved the slightly squashed pomander from his pocket. It still looked presentable, he was glad to see.

"With my regards," he said, holding it out to her.

"Oh—thank you." A blush rose in her cheeks. "That is most kind of you, sir."

"Not at all."

Belatedly, he realized that Miss Daisy was frequently overlooked, not only by himself, but by all the gentlemen who flocked about her sister. Which was a pity. She wasn't a plain girl, truly, but her ordinary brown hair and eyes suffered in comparison with Miss Violet's striking appearance.

"Why, Mr. Plumley," Miss Violet said, sounding a bit put out. "You haven't brought anything for me?"

He turned to her. "You have the entirety of my regard, Miss Thornton."

As the words left his mouth he realized they sounded like the worst kind of puffery, and he winced. Why was it he could never manage to say the right thing to Miss Violet Thornton?

She lifted one brow in a delicate arch. "Ah."

"A gray-haired bank clerk's esteem," Millerton said mockingly. "Surely that is worth several pounds, at least."

The back of Philip's neck prickled with angry heat.

"And what do you have to offer her, Millerton? A pretty face isn't everything."

Thomas Millerton rose, scowling, his hands clenched at his sides. "Is that an insult, sir?"

A tense silence fell. Then Miss Daisy jumped to her feet.

"Mr. Plumley, didn't I hear you've recently come into an inheritance?" she asked, a bit too brightly. "Do sit down, please, the both of you, and let me fetch you some wassail."

Philip and his rival stared at one another for a long moment, eyes narrowed. If he were a brave man, Philip thought, he'd challenge Millerton to a duel.

A brave man possessing ample arrogance, excellent aim, and a pair of dueling pistols, that was. Not to mention a flagrant disregard of the law. He had none of those things.

Best leave duels to the nobility, who could afford them.

"An inheritance?" Miss Violet stared up at Philip, then tugged Millerton's arm. "You heard Daisy. Do sit down."

Slowly, Thomas Millerton subsided. Philip waited for his rival's backside to hit the chair before taking his own seat.

"Here you are," Miss Daisy said, returning with two cups of wassail. Fragrant steam drifted from the surface as she handed the first cup to Philip. "It smells almost as lovely as my pomander."

"Where did you hear of my inheritance?" he asked.

"I believe there was a notice in the Gazette." She smiled at him, then turned to give Millerton his wassail.

Indeed, there had been a notice. And it had been, as Philip recalled, quite accurate as to the dispensation of Great Uncle Henry's penurious estate.

"Daisy, I can't believe you didn't think to mention this information to me," her sister said.

"I didn't think it mattered, overmuch." Miss Daisy's tone was mild, but Philip glimpsed a spark of mischief in her eyes. "Just because Mr. Plumley has come into land and money, it oughtn't change your opinion of him in the least."

"Well, of course not." Miss Violet folded her hands in her lap, then batted her eyelashes at Philip. "But just think of it—our own Mr. Plumley, an heir! What remarkable news."

It was kind of Miss Daisy to try and paint him in a flattering light, and she *had* managed to smooth over a moment of tension, Yet, much as he wanted Miss Violet to continue to gaze at him with open admiration, the untruth did not sit well with him. Land and money sounded well enough, but the reality was something else entirely.

"It would only be remarkable if he'd gotten a title into the bargain." Millerton sounded quite put out, and Philip couldn't help a quick glance of triumph at his rival.

"Did you?" Miss Violet leaned forward. "You ought not to be so very humble, Mr. Plumley. Was it a viscountancy?"

Her avid gaze took all the enjoyment from the charade, and he shifted uncomfortably in his chair. Pleasant as it was to see Millerton squirm, the conversation was showing a side to Miss Violet that he did not find agreeable. At all.

"There was no title," he said, unwilling to support her false assumptions any longer. "The land is nothing but a cottage in Shropshire, and the money is a mere twenty pounds."

"A year?" she asked, with a frown. "Granted, that's not much, but—"

"In total."

"Oh." She dropped her gaze to the profusion of violets arrayed on the table before her. "Then it isn't much of an inheritance, is it? Daisy, why did you even mention it?"

There was no smile on Miss Daisy's face as she glanced first at her sister, then at Philip. "I thought… it might make for interesting conversation."

"Well," Miss Violet let out a thin laugh. "I suppose it was of momentary interest."

"Indeed." Philip's heart contracted to the size of a pea.

He must remember to breathe, even as all his hopes for the future shriveled away to nothing.

Then Miss Daisy brought her pomander up to her nose, closed her eyes, and inhaled. Her lips curved slightly, and a momentary look of joy flitted across her face.

All because of a simple orange stuck with cloves. That he had given her.

Suddenly, Philip felt as though a veil had been ripped from his eyes. Or even, macabre as it might seem, as though the executioner's hood had been pulled from his head.

The brightness was painful, yet who did not welcome a reprieve from a deadly future? Especially when a far better one had been beside it all along?

Miss Daisy opened her eyes. Seeing him watching her, her brows drew together in remorse.

"I am sorry, Mr. Plumley," she said. "I thought my sister would find your news of more importance."

He gave her a rueful shake of his head. "Unfortunately, some people can't see what's right in front of their faces."

Such as the fact that Miss Daisy Thornton had been his constant ally—even selflessly promoting him to her sister when, he suspected, she had formed an attachment to him of her own.

At least, he greatly hoped it was the case. The wife he'd been looking for had been under the Thornton's roof all along—even if it wasn't whom he expected.

"Is your father available?" he asked.

She stiffened. "I believe he's in his study. Do you... wish to speak with him?"

"I do."

A desolate expression crossed her face and she glanced at her older sister, who was ignoring the both of them to shamelessly flirt with Millerton.

"Violet is always the lucky one," she said softly.

"I think luck is overrated." Philip leaned toward her. "I believe you've guessed that I mean to ask your father's permission to court his daughter."

"Yes," she said unhappily. "I wish you much joy, Mr. Plumley."

"Here, now." He couldn't bear the misery in her eyes, and reached out to catch her fingers in his. "Why are you assuming I'm asking for his oldest daughter's hand? He has two, you know."

She met his gaze, and he heard her breath catch.

"You don't mean—you're not asking for *me*?" Her voice ended on a squeak, and she blushed.

In that moment, he found her far more beautiful than her sister had ever been. He didn't need to pursue some perfect ideal—especially when that ideal's character fell so far short of his expectations.

"Asking for you is precisely what I'm planning to do." He squeezed her hand, his own heart giving a little jolt. "That is, if you don't mind."

"But, why?" She shot a look at her sister, then back to them, confusion in her eyes.

"You are kind, Miss Daisy Thornton, and generous of spirit. Cheerful, and, if I recall correctly, light on your feet." Strange, that he'd almost forgotten how well they'd danced together.

He supposed he'd been so consumed with thoughts of Miss Violet that he'd put her sister's accomplishments out of his mind. It was not Miss Daisy he'd been smitten with, after all. And yet, here he was, holding her hand and staring into her eyes, and it all felt perfectly right.

"Mr. Plumley! Are you making overtures to my sister?" Miss Violet sounded horrified. "I insist you release her hand at once."

Instead, he lifted it and pressed a kiss on the back.

"To new beginnings," he said.

Miss Daisy's smile was radiant. "And the very best of fortune in the coming year."

She met his gaze, and he had a sudden flash of surety that they would share that same, knowing smile together, over and over, until his hair was gray in truth. That their years would unspool behind them, shining and contented, in the light of every new day.

~*~

OTHER WORKS

Discover all of Anthea's books~

~NOVELS~
Sonata for a Scoundrel
Mistress of Melody
Fortune's Flower
To Heal a Heart

~COLLECTIONS~
Noble Holidays
Passport to Romance boxed set
Kisses & Rogues
Regency Sweets
Music of the Heart boxed set
Noble Pleasures

~SHORTER WORKS~
The Duke's Christmas

To Wed the Earl
A Lady's Choice
A Lord's Chance
The Viscount's Secret
Waltzed

ABOUT THE AUTHOR

A *USA Today* bestselling author and two-time RITA nominee, Anthea Lawson was named "one of the new stars of historical romance" by *Booklist*. Her books have received starred reviews in *Library Journal* and *Publishers Weekly*.

Anthea splits her time between sunny southern California and the lush, enchanted forests of the Pacific Northwest. In addition to writing historical romance, Anthea plays the Irish fiddle and pens bestselling, award-winning YA urban fantasy as Anthea Sharp.

Find out about all her books at anthealawson.com, and join her mailing list, tinyletter.com/AntheaLawson, for a free story, plus all the news about upcoming releases and reader perks!

www.ingramcontent.com/pod-product-compliance
Lightning Source LLC
Chambersburg PA
CBHW010517100726
47903CB00009B/2784